Olly Spellmaker
and the Sulky Smudge

Susan Price

Illustrated by David Roberts

MACMILLAN CHILDREN'S BOOKS

First published 2003 by Macmillan Children's Books

First edition published 2004 by Macmillan Children's Books
a division of Macmillan Publishers Limited
20 New Wharf Road, London N1 9RR
Basingstoke and Oxford
www.panmacmillan.com

Associated companies throughout the world

ISBN 0 330 41582 4

1 3 5 7 9 8 6 4 2

A CIP catalogue record for this book is available from
the British Library.

Typeset by Nigel Hazle
Printed and bound in Great Britain by Mackays of Chatham plc, Kent

Olly Spellmaker and the Sulky Smudge

Susan Price started writing and telling stories when she was very young – and was winning prizes for it from the age of fourteen. Her first novel, *The Devil's Piper*, was bought by a publisher when she was sixteen. Since then, she has had lots of jobs and written many books for children and young adults, including *The Sterkarm Handshake* (which won the Guardian Children's Fiction Award) and *The Ghost Drum* (which won the Carnegie Medal).

Visit Susan Price's website at
www.susanprice.org.uk

Also by Susan Price from Macmillan

Olly Spellmaker and the Hairy Horror

1. A Job offer

From: o.spellmaker@geist.co.uk
Subject: Need your help . . .

O Alex, little mate, little friend.
Be a precious angel and meet me for a nosh and a natter.

It's always good to get an email from a friend, but Alex wasn't sure about this one. He did like Olly, but . . . Well, she was a bit embarrassing. She was a witch, for one thing, and she kept trying to persuade Alex that he was a witch too, when he didn't want to be a witch. Even if he *could* twingle.

From: Alex34@spruce.co.uk
Subject: Wot's this about?

It had better be good.

From: o.spellmaker@geist.co.uk

Subject: Money, money, money . . .

It's about things that go crash, bang, wallop in the night. C'mon. Be a friend. Meet me in town, by the fountain, four-fifteen. I'll give you a lift home.

This sounded to Alex like more witchy stuff. He really didn't want to get involved – but they did owe Olly a favour. When their house had been invaded by a Hairy Bogle that decorated at the dead of night, it had been Olly who had saved them from it.

From: Alex34@spruce.co.uk

Subject: OK.

This had better be good . . .

The fountain stood at the end of the market place, by Boots and Woolworths. It was a big white thing, fancy as a wedding cake, carved with rearing horses that had fishes' tails, and women dressed like ancient Greeks with jugs

on their heads, and dolphins, bunches of
grapes, garlands of flowers – it was just
dripping with carving. Not with water any
more, though. It had been dry for years,
though the two big basins for the water to fall
into were still there,
and the water-
spouts in the
shape of chubby
babies' heads.
But it made a
wonderful meeting

place. People splitting up to go to different shops would say, 'Meet you by the fountain in ten minutes.' There were always people sitting on its steps and on the edges of its basins, waiting for other people.

Alex quickly spotted Olly, leaning against one of the fountain's basins. Her short, fat figure stood out, especially against the white stone, because she was wearing her black motorcycle leathers and boots. She didn't seem to have her helmet with her. When she saw him, she spread her arms and called, 'Ally! Blessings be, little pal of mine!'

Alex cringed and looked round to see if anyone was laughing at them, but none of the passing shoppers seemed to have taken any notice. 'Tone it down,' he said. Her hair was still impenetrably black and shiny, he saw, and she was still making up her eyes with thick black lines, like an ancient Egyptian, though she'd left off the blue lipstick today. There was still a silver stud through the middle of her bottom lip and another through her eyebrow. He looked to see if, as usual, she was wearing a moon earring in one ear and a sun earring in the other. To his amazement, he saw that her earrings were dangling silver skeletons. They had tiny joints and waggled their arms and legs as she moved her head. It was hard to stop watching them.

'Come on, quick step,' Olly said. 'We got places to go, people to see.'

Alex followed her as she started off down the street. 'Where are we going and for how long? I've got to get home for six.'

'No worries,' Olly said. 'You worry too much, little pal. The Goddess looks after all!'

She led him downhill, to the small car park by the library. He looked for her big motorbike, a gleaming black-and-silver machine with 'Stormrider' painted on the fuel tank. He was half looking forward to a ride on it and a bit nervous about it at the same time. What was he going to do for a helmet?

Did Olly have one in his size? But he couldn't see a motorbike in the car park.

Olly went up to a little Vauxhall Nova, a very old one, and started unlocking it. Alex gaped. The bonnet was covered in rust spots and one door was light blue, while the rest of the car was maroon. 'Is this *yours*?' he said.

'Your carriage awaits!' Olly left the passenger door open for him and went round to the driver's door.

When they were both inside, he said, 'What happened to Stormrider?'

'*Hors de combat*,' Olly said, as she started the car and reversed out of the parking place. 'A cracked piston. Humungous job, and the garage geezers are demanding oodles of spondulicks before Storm rides again.'

As they drove through town, Alex said sadly, 'I wish you'd talk English.'

'Storm's off the road,' Olly translated. 'She can be fixed, but it's going to cost big bucks. That's why I need your help, little pal. Got a job. It's tricky but I need the readies pronto. So please, please, be a brick, and render assistance, or it's Shanks's pony *pour moi* when my friend wants this car back.'

'What is the job?' Alex asked.

'A-ha! Been practising your witchcraft?'

'I don't want to be a witch, I told you.'

'But you are a witch. You twingle. Don't fight it, petal.'

'Just because I get – get –' Alex couldn't think of another word for it, 'get twingles doesn't mean I *have* to be a witch. I want to work with computers.'

'Nothing says a witch can't work with computers,' Olly said. 'Some of the best do, these days. Still, I won't nag.'

They were still driving through town, along busy roads. As they pulled up at traffic lights, Alex tried again. 'What kind of job is it?'

'We'll be there soon,' Olly said.

'Are you going to tell me what the job is?'

'Not till we're there.'

Annoyed, Alex said, 'Why do you wear motorcycle leathers to drive a stupid beat-up old Nova?'

'I'm just a fool for black leather. It's so witchy, darling.'

The long, straight road lined with big houses turned into a long, straight road passing between fields and hedges. Alex realized that he knew it. He'd often driven along it with his father when they were going to the Edge, a piece of wild, open country where you could wander through woodlands or scramble up red sandstone cliffs. But Olly drove past the turning for the Edge and continued on, driving fast along a dual carriageway. They passed a sign, painted in dark green and gold. It said, 'The Olde Manor Inne'. An arrow pointed to the right. Olly slowed down, and turned right, into an entrance almost hidden with overgrown bushes and trees.

Alex leaned forward, peering through the

windscreen. All he could see was thick greenery leaning in from either side. There was no sign of any building at all. The lane curved and a gap in the hedge let them see a green pond with ducks swimming on it and then another curve brought them to the Inne.

It was a very old, timbered house. The timbers, some curved, some straight, were weathered to a soft, silvery grey. Between the timbers, the plasterwork was a pale ochre, while above, the uneven roof was of dark

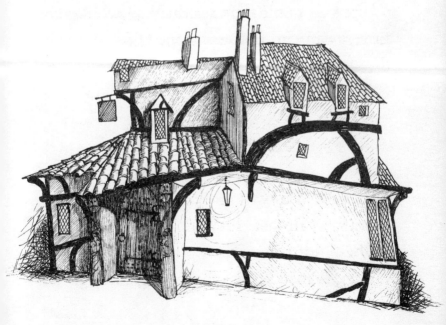

slate, grown with orangey lichens and tufts of green moss. The glass of the small windows seemed black, as if the house were full of darkness, but the diamond-shaped panes flashed brightly where they caught the sun. The door was set back within an arched porch, but Alex could see that, in the shadows of the porch, the door was small and narrow, with a massive beam above it and another at either side. The dark wood of the door was studded with many rows of big nail-heads.

'Look at that,' Olly said. 'Did you ever see a more haunted house?'

2. The Olde Manor Inne

They got out of the Nova and stood looking at the old Inne. It was very quiet. A couple of cars were parked in the small car park, but no one was about. The busy road seemed a long way off and the traffic could hardly be heard. Instead there was a soft, insistent sound, like falling rain, which Alex soon realized was the sound of the wind passing through the upper branches of the trees. And it was getting dark. He felt a need to look over his shoulder.

'Built in thirteen-umpty-plonk,' Olly said. 'Leans a bit, but hasn't fallen down yet. Come and have a butcher's inside.'

She led the way into the little porch. As he stepped under the heavy timbers, and on to the uneven, buckled, red tiles, Alex felt the age of the place press on him. The beams that framed the door were carved with odd little figures. Women with bare breasts held swords and turned into trees below their waists. Ugly little faces screwed up their eyes and thrust out long tongues or showed fangs. Funny things to have carved on your front door, he thought.

Olly shouldered open the heavy door and Alex followed her into a tiny hallway, floored with warped wooden boards that tilted up and down under his feet. There were even gaps between some of them. Dark wood was everywhere, absorbing the light until everything was dim and shadowy. The walls were all of dark wood and dark beams crossed the ceiling. In front of them rose a narrow staircase of polished, black wood, with a tall stairpost carved into the shape of a seated hound. The steps were worn into hollows and they sloped and slanted. It was as if the age of the place – the sheer weight of all those years, all those centuries – had pushed everything slightly out of true.

A pleased voice said, 'Olly! Hello!' Startled, Alex looked to his right, and saw a tiny reception desk made of dark, polished wood, but obviously much more modern than the rest of the house. Behind it, a young woman smiled.

Olly leaned on the desk in her motorcycle leathers.

'Allow me to introduce my glamorous assistant.' She waved a theatrical hand. 'Give us a twirl, Alex.'

The young woman behind the desk leaned forward to see him. 'Hello Alex,' she called and waved. 'I'm Lisa.'

Alex, who didn't like being called a

glamorous assistant, couldn't decide whether to scowl or smile, and didn't have time to make up his mind before Olly said, 'Off you go and have a nozzuk. See what you make of the old place.'

'What?' Alex said. 'Just – wander round? On my own?' It was something, he felt, that was likely to get him into trouble.

'It's cool,' Olly said. 'Everybody knows me here.'

'They don't know *me*,' Alex said.

'Don't be a worry-bead. If anybody collars you, just say you're with Olly. Now skedaddle, go on, git.'

'What am I supposed to be looking for?' Alex asked.

'Oh – boggles, bloody-bones, demons, night-bats, bargeists, scrags, breaknecks, mum-pokers, melch-dicks, swaiths, gringes, shag-foals, yeth-hounds, nisses – anything of that sort. See if you get a twingle.'

A twingle was what Olly called that feeling

Alex got when he felt as though there was something behind him. It was more than a nervy feeling that made him want to turn round, though. Olly had taught him to recognize the sense of very quiet noise going on somewhere. A sort of crackling and buzzing that he felt more than heard. It set his teeth on edge slightly and made his hands uncomfortable, as if the palms and thumbs were itching. The twingle.

'On my own? Thanks a lot.'

'Oh, you're not scared of a few old boggleboes and chittifaces,' Olly said. 'Go on with you. Have a good gander and then come back – and Lisa and me'll debrief you.'

Lisa laughed at this, which Alex thought was rude and unkind of her, and he was glad to leave their company. He decided to look upstairs first. 'This had better be worth it,' he said to Olly, as he started to climb.

At the top of the steep, uneven stairs was a long, dark corridor, all heavy beams and black, wooden panelling. The windows were small and let in only faint, grey light. His footsteps rang out sharply on the bare floorboards as he walked towards the far end. To his left was a line of secretive closed doors, with numbers on them. Anything might come out of them, he thought, imagining a chittiface or a boggleboe suddenly sticking out its head to demand room service. Then he realized that he wasn't really scared at all. He just thought that he ought to feel scared.

He stood by a window to think about it and

16

looked out at a grey, wintry yard, with little trees in pots and a few damp tables and chairs. He remembered when Hairy Bill had been haunting his own house. All the time he'd been half aware of a sort of buzzing in his head, an itching in his palms. Then his mother had invited Olly in, and Olly had told him that was why a haunted house was called 'an unquiet house'. But he felt no twingle here. The place was old, it was dark, it was silent. It seemed fit to be a haunted house in every way. But it was a quiet house.

He went back along the corridor and down the stairs. No one was at the reception desk, so he wandered along the corridor towards the back of the house, feeling a little guilty, as if he was doing something he shouldn't. There were odd little twisted doorways opening off into tiny, dark little rooms, furnished with tables and benches. In one, a coal fire was burning in a grate.

He pushed through a door into a much

larger room that had been made into a bar. Great supporting timbers rose up from the floor to the ceiling, which was crossed with black beams. There was Olly, sitting at a table with a half pint of beer. 'Chips coming soon!' she said, the silver skeletons dancing in her ears. 'Park your bum and tell me what you've gleaned.'

'You're driving,' Alex said, looking at the half pint.

'Half a pint of Throgmorton's Fancy and a plate of chips won't put me over the limit,' she said. 'What d'you think of the little grey home in the west?'

Alex sat down opposite her on a long settle. 'It's not haunted.'

'No more it is. I knew you had the knack.'

Alex was annoyed. 'What have you dragged me over here for, if it's not haunted?'

At that moment, Lisa came from somewhere in the shadows beside the bar, carrying a tray with two bowls of chips on it.

She set it down on their table with a smile.

'The infant phenomenon,' Olly said to her, 'wants to know what we're doing here when the place isn't haunted by so much as a will o' the wisp?'

'Ah,' said Lisa, leaning on the edge of the table. 'Well, you see, Alex – the place isn't haunted. But I'd like it to be.'

3. Ghost-finder General

'Take it from me,' Alex said, 'ghosts are more trouble than they're worth. You think they're going to be fun, but they keep you awake at night and wake you up early in the morning and redecorate when you're not looking and tidy up all the time and move things so you can't find 'em. You get fed up of it.'

'That's bogles,' Olly said. 'Not every ghost is a bogle.'

'And this isn't fun, Alex,' Lisa said. 'This is business.'

'You can't make ghosts work,' Alex said. 'Well, you can't make 'em do what you want 'em to do, anyway.'

'Alex,' Olly said, 'they don't want ghosts

whipping up soufflés or mixing martinis. Good chips, by the way.' She had peeled the top off a little tub of tomato ketchup and was picking chips up in her fingers, dipping them in the ketchup and eating them.

'The idea,' Lisa said, 'is to have "Ghost Evenings". Y'know, a special deal – evening meal, bed and breakfast – but bed in a haunted room. That's extra, of course. But even if you just have the regular evening meal, bed and breakfast, you still have a chance to see a ghost – in this amazing, ancient, moated, half-timbered, thirteenth-century, *haunted*, manor house. I was thinking,' she said enthusiastically to Olly, 'of having special evenings with a seance. And setting up all that doo-dah the psychical researchers have – y'know, infra-red cameras and machines to show the sudden drop in temperature. A real ghost hunt. Give the punters something for their money.'

'Only trouble is,' Olly said, still eating

chips, 'not a sausage of a ghost. Or even the ghost of a sausage. Not so much as a groan in a dark corner.'

Lisa threw herself into a chair. 'I'm not doing the business I should. I'm away from the road, so I don't get the passing trade, even with the sign. I put everything into this business: all my savings, sold my house.' She leaned forward again. 'If it fails, I'm flat broke.'

Olly stopped eating chips and reached out and took Lisa's hands, pulling them away from her face. She smiled at her. Alex sat watching, thinking how terrible it was to be grown up and have worries like that. He didn't think his parents had any such worries. He hoped not.

'People expect a place like this to be haunted,' Lisa said. 'That's what I get asked, again and again. "I bet you've got a ghost," people say. They're disappointed when you have to say there isn't one.'

'Tell them there is,' Alex said. 'Make up a story.' It seemed the obvious solution to him.

'But I had a ghost club here last year,' Lisa said. 'That's what gave me the idea. They asked if they could come and set up their monitors and keep watch all night – and, well, they bought a lot of beer and breakfasts, so I was happy to have them. But they didn't find a thing. No ghosts, they said. And it was reported in the local papers. "Seven-Hundred-Year-Old Manor Inne Not Haunted." That didn't help business. It fell off even more after that. Olly, you've *got* to get me a ghost!'

'And I will,' Olly said. 'That's why I've brought along my little pal.'

They both looked at Alex.

'Don't look at me,' he said. 'The only ghost I ever met, I was glad to see the back of.' He nodded at Olly. '*She*'s the one who knows all about ghosts. Why drag me into it?'

Lisa looked at Olly. 'I could do with two or three,' she said. 'Maybe more if things went well. Then I could offer more than one haunted bedroom.'

'Well, I looked into it a bit,' Olly said. 'Problem is, when I get to hear about a ghost, it's usually because people want rid of some pestilential poltergeist or heinous haunt. Something that chucks cans of pilchards about and starts fires or opens all the windows when it's pouring. Not the sort of thing you want around when you're trying to run a business.'

'You must know of some nice, quiet ghosts,' Lisa said.

'Well, no. 'Cos if people are happy with their ghost, they don't call yours truly. But then I remembered my little pal, Al. I thought, I bet there's a lad who can point us in the direction of a few ghosts.'

'I don't know *any* ghosts!' Alex said. 'I knew this was going to be a waste of time.'

'Oh, Alex, cogitate,' Olly said. 'Ponder. Ruminate. You mean, you don't know of a haunted house?'

That set things moving in Alex's head. 'Come to think of it – my old school was haunted.'

'Bullseye!' Olly said. 'In my experience, if you want to know where to find a ghost, ask the local kids.'

'What was your school haunted by?' Lisa asked.

'A green lady,' Alex said. 'She used to walk through the hall, in a green dress, wringing her hands and crying.'

'What for?' Lisa asked.

'I don't know,' Alex said.

'Did you ever see her?'

'No,' Alex said. 'I was never in the school hall at night. The caretaker was supposed to have seen her, but if you asked him about it, he said, "I'll green-lady yer if you don't watch out!"'

'There, you see,' Olly said, finishing her own bowl of chips and starting, absent-mindedly, on Alex's. 'We've got a lead already. I bet if you asked about at school, you'd hear about a dozen more.'

Lisa took a chip from the bowl and tapped Alex lightly on either shoulder with it. 'I dub you Ghost-finder General!' Then she ate the chip.

4. School Hall Screams

It was twenty-five minutes to midnight and, instead of being warm, comfortable and asleep in his bed, Alex was awake and tired in the draughty hall of his old primary school. Only one set of lights was switched on and the big, long room was depressingly dim and shadowy. The windows were covered with long, black curtains, and Alex was unhappily aware that it was pitch dark outside and anything or anyone could be standing just on the other side of the glass, hidden by the drapes. The only company he had in this place was a witch. A mad witch, at that.

She was quite happy. She'd brought along a couple of camping stools, an electric kettle and a cardboard box holding tea, milk, sugar, biscuits and sandwiches. There she sat, on a stool, dunking biscuits into a plastic cup of tea, her face-piercings and earrings glinting in the light. At least she wasn't wearing her biking leathers. It was jeans, trainers and a big warm fleece tonight. All black, of course.

Alex was pacing up and down. 'What if there's nothing here? What if nothing happens?'

'Oh, there's something here all right, me old china. You know there is.'

He did. He could feel it – a faint buzzing in his head, an ever-so-slight itching in his palms.

When he'd been a pupil at this school, before he'd met Olly, he'd always thought that he disliked the hall because – well, it wasn't a very attractive place. And because the assemblies held there were always so boring. He hadn't known what the faint, irritable buzzing, or the slight itching meant then. Now he knew that it meant the place was haunted.

'If she doesn't stalk the midnight hour off her own bat,' Olly said, 'I'll summon her with mystic incantations. Want a biccie?'

They were chocolate ones. Alex went over to the camp-stool that had been set up for him, sat down, and accepted a cup of tea.

'Plenty of sandwiches,' Olly said. 'Egg. Ham. Peanut butter.'

'How long are we going to wait?'

'We'll give her till midnight. After that, I'll make a nuisance of myself.'

'You're good at that,' Alex said.

'It's a talent to be cherished. Actually,

ghosts usually show up around one in the morning, but I'd like to get *some* kip. And I gave my solemn oath to your parents that I wouldn't keep you out all night.'

'I don't know how you got them to agree at all.'

'My persuasive powers are very great,' Olly said. 'I keep talking until people realize I'm not going to go away or shut up until they give in.' She sucked the chocolate thoughtfully from a biscuit. 'I'm a sort of occult double-glazing salesman.'

Alex nodded. It sounded about right.

'The caretaker, now. It only took me an hour to wear him down. And the fiver I slipped him for his trouble.'

The caretaker had already been round on a tour of inspection and had taken tea and biscuits with Olly. Alex had hung back, leaning on the hall's stage. He didn't like the caretaker, who'd always been bad tempered when he'd known him, but the man was cheerful enough with Olly. Typical, Alex thought. Grown-ups stuck together.

'My dog never will come in here,' the caretaker had said, nodding toward the door where his dog waited. 'If I carry him in, he whines and runs away.'

'A hopeful sign!' Olly had said. 'Where does the spook usually shove its mug in, do you know?'

The caretaker pointed towards the windows, with their long curtains. 'It's supposed to walk along there, by the windows. A woman in a long green dress, twisting her hands together and crying. That's what people say. I've never seen it meself.'

'Have you felt its presence?' Olly asked.

The big man shrugged. 'Well . . . People put ideas into your head and then you imagine things, don't you? No, I've never really seen or heard or felt anything. Well, thanks for the tea. Lock up when you leave. G'night.'

That had been about half-past nine, not long after Alex had helped Olly carry in the stools and kettle, just as the last of the evening-class people were leaving. Ever since then – for two hours - they'd been sitting there, in the big, empty building, measuring the time in cars passing by on the road and floorboards creaking.

'I did what you said,' Alex said. 'I asked around at school. About ghosts.'

'And?' Olly asked.

'You were right. People know about loads of them. There's a blue lady haunts the Black Horse –'

'We won't get her. The pub'll want to hang on to her and ghosts are usually happy in pubs.'

'Oh. Well, there's a white lady haunts the towpath by the canal.'

'She's a prospect.'

'And there's a—' He broke off because Olly had raised her hand, warning him to listen.

At once, he moved his stool closer to hers. The buzzing in his head, now he was paying attention, was that little bit louder and more insistent, and he wanted to scratch the palms of his hands. There was a faint sound too: a muttering, a breathy sighing, just loud enough to be heard.

Olly was looking towards the far end of the hall, at the curtains there. Alex looked at the same place. Something was moving. He couldn't quite see what, but his heart gave a big jump and his breath caught. Something, in the shadows of the corner and the darkness of the curtain, was swaying, shifting.

It came into focus. A woman stood there. A tall woman in a long, dark green dress.

'Olly!' Alex said, in a strangulated voice.

Olly gripped his arm. 'Ssh. It's only a ghost.'

That was all right for *her* to say. The only other ghost Alex had met had been the bogle Hairy Bill, and Hairy Bill had turned very nasty. Alex wanted to run away, but he was scared to be on his own in the empty school.

The ghost walked beside the curtained windows, coming closer to where they stood. They heard the tread of her feet on a wooden floor. Her hands were pressed together and she moaned and then raised both hands to her eyes, groaning. The groan was so sorrowful and lonely, it sent a pang through Alex's heart and he shivered.

The hall was colder. The woman came on towards them, the heels of her shoes clacking on the floor and her skirt dragging. She moaned and wailed softly to herself, now twisting her hands in front of her, as if she was washing them, now raising them to her face. All the edges of her – her dark dress and her dark hair – faded into the shadows, but her white face stood out clearly. She had very dark eyes and very red lips.

The ghostly woman came as close as Alex thought he could bear – he thought if she took

one more step, he really would run. Olly stood and said, 'Spirit, speak! I command you!'

The ghost stopped short and turned her white face in their direction. She stared at them a moment and then said, 'How dare you speak to me in that tone of voice?'

'Oh, get off your high horse,' Olly said. 'I'm a witch – Olly Spellmaker – and I'll speak to any ghost as I please. This here is Alex.'

As the ghost continued to stare, Alex said, 'Hello!' He didn't know whether he should have spoken or not. He'd never been introduced to a ghost before.

'Go!' cried the ghost, flinging out an arm. 'Leave me to my misery.' And she raised her head, drew breath for another moan and made to sweep on.

'Why be miserable?' Olly asked. 'Get it all off your chest, that's the business. You'll feel better for it.'

'N-o-o-o-o!' cried the ghost and the air

thrilled to her voice. She put her hands to her face again. 'Oh my sins, my unconfessed and unforgiven sins.' A shrill, wild note in her voice seemed to set a strong, cold wind blowing through the hall. Even the lights flickered and dimmed. The ghost wailed again and it was as if the sound touched Alex on a nerve. Tears came to his eyes. Poor ghost. Poor, sad thing.

'Bung the old confession our way, then,' Olly said. 'We're all ears. And we're game; we'll forgive.'

'No! No!' The ghost sobbed into her hands. 'I cannot bear to speak – to think – of my sins.'

'Please yourself,' Olly said. Alex nudged her. He thought she was being very unsympathetic. Olly glanced down at him, but said, 'Here's the deal. I can send you on to the next place, if you like, if that's your bag.'

The ghost clenched her hands together, threw back her head and cried, in a throbbing

voice, 'Not with my sins, not with my sins –
no, no!'

'Fair enough,' Olly said. 'Then how's about
a change of scene? Pack it in here, and
decamp to a nice country house. Lovely décor.
Real fire. Best ale on tap.'

The ghost lost her dramatic pose, lowered
her head and stood quite naturally. 'Is that
allowed?'

'There's no rule says you've got to stay here
till Doomscrack,' Olly said.

'But here is the place of my sins – here,
where my house stood. How can I leave?'

'Why stay here, in a draughty school hall
that ain't had a lick of paint in twenty years,
surrounded by nasty little herberts like this
one –'

'Hey!' Alex said.

'When you can come and haunt in the sort
of style you're used to?'

'I am tempted,' the ghost said. 'But how
would I get there?'

'You don't have to hire a removal van,' Olly said. 'Leave it to me. A day or two hence, me lover, when I've tied some knots in a few other loose ends, I'll go to your new home, make with the old mystic passes, and call you over. You just be ready.'

'What if I don't like it when I get there?' the ghost asked.

'No contracts, no ties,' Olly said. 'If, when you get there, you don't like the look of the curtains or the niff of the air-freshener, you can come right back here.'

'But I shan't know how!'

'Easy-peasy,' Olly said. 'I'll call you over the first time, and you'll be surprised how quickly you pick it up. Once you know the way, you can come back here any time you like, for a visit.'

'Truly?' said the ghost.

'Some ghosts dodge about all over the shop, every night of the year,' Olly said.

'I never knew,' the ghost said. 'What a silly.

Well. What shall I do now? Shall I carry on here in the meantime?'

Olly shrugged. 'You can if you like.'

'Do I have to?'

'Do you want to?' Olly asked.

The ghost swung from side to side, looking about her. 'Quite honestly – no. Who ever sees me? At least when my old place was still here, I used to have the odd word with my descendants or a housemaid. A little appreciation.'

'Have a few days off and kick back, then,' Olly said. 'I should.'

The ghost thought about it and nodded. 'I will. But I might as well finish off tonight.' She cast back her head, put the back of her hand to her forehead and wailed, 'Oh my sins, my unforgiven sins!' Down the hall she went, wringing her hands and sobbing. Just as she reached the far wall, she turned, said, 'Bye-bye!' – and walked through the bricks.

Olly turned to pack up her biscuits, stools

and kettle. 'Well, that was a doddle and no mistake.'

Alex helped Olly carry her things out to the battered little Nova. 'What were her sins?' he asked.

'Do I look like somebody who cares?'

'You should have asked her.'

'No chance!' Olly said. 'She'd have wept and wailed all night, and we'd still be here at dawn's early light. Trust me, I know. A drama-queen in life is a drama-queen in death.'

'But it might have been something really good.' Alex tried to think of the worst possible sin someone could commit. 'Murder!'

'Knowing her type, she probably forgot to put the cat out one night. Still, good going. Stormrider is one ghost nearer being back on the road. Now where did you say this White Lady was?'

5. Canal Creeps

They hadn't come far from the street, with its houses, shops and passing cars. Olly, dressed in jeans and fleece again, had led the way down some steps to a canal towpath, and then along the path for perhaps ten minutes. The traffic on the road still hummed quite loudly.

The path had brought them to a stretch of open ground. During the day, it was probably full of people kicking balls about and walking dogs, but at nearly midnight, it was dark, cold, quiet and lonely. It didn't seem, to Alex, a very good place to be. Especially when he only had Olly to protect him. What use would she be?

'Anybody might come along,' he said. 'Murderers. Robbers.'

Olly was sitting under the bridge on her campstool. An electric kettle was no good to her here, but she had a thermos flask, some biscuits and some sandwiches. 'It'd take a brainless murderer or robber to hang about down here! There's nobody to murder or rob!'

'There's us,' Alex said.

'Ah, but they don't know we're here, do they? I forgot to put that advert in the *Murderer's Gazette*.'

'Oh, shut up,' Alex said.

'And if I was a robber, I wouldn't lug me cosh all the way down here, under a canal bridge. I'd go to pub car parks, places like that, where I know there are going to be lots of half-cut people with money in their pockets.'

'Maybe they're very stupid robbers,' Alex muttered.

'Well, then: we'll talk 'em into giving us *their* money. Do you feel a twingle?'

'No,' Alex said.

'Concentrate. I think she's coming.'

Alex did feel it then – or was it his imagination, prompted by Olly's words? He wasn't sure. But it seemed to him that his hands started to itch and the night turned colder. He shivered and crept closer to Olly. She pointed to the canal, just at the point where it came under the bridge.

Alex looked. Something bulged from the water. It moved towards the bank and reached to climb out. Something large. Not a dog.

Cold moved up his back and prickled in his hair. A woman was crawling from the canal. Water streamed from her long hair as she dragged herself on to the bank. Somehow, it seemed especially horrible that she crawled and dragged herself, on all fours, with her hair wet and trailing. She stood and he saw that she was dressed in a long, soaked, white dress that was plastered to her gaunt body. Water poured from it.

She looked from side to side and saw them.

Alex nearly jumped off the ground when her eyes met his and flashed silver, as if with fierce interest. Slowly, she turned towards them, trailing weed and streams of water, took one step and then another, reaching out her hands as she came.

Alex felt an icy cold streaming from the top of his head, but when the ghost gave a long, throbbing wail that echoed under the bridge and sawed on his nerves, his heart lurched and he thought he might fall over. Olly gripped his arm. 'Get used to it,' she said. 'That's what ghosts do. It's all show.'

'Poor, unhappy mortals,' said the ghost, her face white and staring. Water poured down past her eyes and mouth. 'Come with me, come away with me, away from the pain and trials of life, away from—'

'Lighten up,' Olly said. She put down her thermos and stood. 'Let's not dance around the mulberry bush. I've come to make you an offer, darlin'.'

The White Lady drew back in surprise, splashing water about. Then she gathered herself and came on again. 'Come to me, sink down in the water with me, breathe your last—'

'Give over,' Olly said, 'and listen for a minute.'

The White Lady folded her arms, turned

her back, and tapped her foot. 'Nothing goes right for me. I wish I was dead.'

From behind Olly, Alex whispered, 'She is.'

'You are,' Olly said.

'Figure of speech!' the White Lady snapped. 'Have I got to watch every word I say? Everybody picks on me, about every little thing. It's not fair.'

Alex felt like giggling and pressed his face against Olly's back to stop himself.

'Spirit, I command thee!' Olly suddenly said, in a loud, firm voice. The White Lady's head jerked up, snapping out her long hair and splattering water in all directions. 'Listen to me. I can send you on from this place, to your deserved rest. Is that what you wish?'

'Oh – what's the point?' the White Lady said. 'It'd be just the same there. If your face doesn't fit, it's no use trying. Nothing ever goes right for me. I can't—'

'Yes, all right, all right,' Olly said. 'How about this then? How about moving to a nice, warm, dry country house, where you can do your haunting in comfort? Appear in bedrooms, depress the paying guests. Drip through the conference rooms, cast a pall on the wedding feast, that sort of thing. You'd be good at that.'

Alex, peering from behind Olly, thought

the White Lady perked up a little. Her head half turned, anyway. She seemed, for a moment, interested. But she said, 'It wouldn't be any good. No, I'll stay here, knocking meself out where nobody ever comes, and when they do, they turn out to be ruddy witches who—'

'Yeah, yeah, blah, blah, right enough,' Olly said. 'How about coming and giving it a bash anyway? You can always come back here and sulk if you don't like it.'

'Just forget me,' said the ghost. 'Everybody does.'

'Oh, Goddess help us,' Olly said. 'Do you want me to beg? Well, get this, White Madam. I'm a witch, I don't beg. Pack up your old bike-frames and bedsteads, or whatever you've got down there, because in a couple of days I'll be summoning you to your new haunt and you'll be going. OK?'

'I don't suppose it matters what I think,' said the ghost.

'No, doesn't matter a spit,' Olly said. 'Alex, get the things. We're going.'

The ghost swayed about from foot to foot. 'I might as well get back in the water, then,' she said.

Alex had folded up his stool and was hugging the sandwich box. 'Yeah, you might as well,' he said.

The ghost marched back to the spot where it had climbed out of the canal and jumped in again. She hardly made a splash.

'You were a bit nasty to her,' Alex said, as he and Olly walked back to the road.

'Well, what a pain,' Olly said. 'Typical water ghost, all dank and depressing. They get on my wick.'

'Will she be very good for the hotel? I mean, do they want to depress their guests?'

'An experience is what people want from a ghost,' Olly said. 'The cold shivers, the creeping horrors – I think the White Lady'll do very well. Do you want to come and see me move 'em in?'

Alex decided that he did. 'Aren't you going to look for some more?'

'Two'll do to be going on with. Should put one of Stormrider's wheels back on the road, at least. But if you hear of any more ghosts, give me a tinkle.'

6. A Grey Blob

Alex heard of another that very night – or, rather, he felt it.

'I won't come in,' Olly said, when she dropped him off outside his house. 'It's too late.'

It was nearly one o'clock in the morning. Alex felt tired, but also grown-up and important. He waved goodbye to Olly, and went up his garden path.

His mother opened the door before he got there. 'Is that Olly?' she said. 'Come away in. It's long past your bedtime. Do you want something before you go up?'

'No,' Alex said. 'Olly had sandwiches and biscuits as usual.'

'So she's feeding you rubbish as well as

keeping you up till all hours.' She shut and locked the door. 'I'm not at all sure I should let you go to these places with her.'

'Oh Mum,' Alex said, as he went up the stairs. 'Don't be boring.' It was funny how keen he felt about Olly's expeditions as soon as his mother objected to them.

It was as he stood in the bathroom, brushing his teeth, that he began to feel there was something behind him. He twingled.

His toothbrush still in his mouth, Alex turned round. There was nothing behind him except the bathroom door and the towels hanging on it. But the room felt colder than usual.

He went along the landing to his bedroom and undressed. All the time he did so, he could feel the room

growing colder. And the twingle was still with him.

He was wishing Olly was there, when he thought: Why don't I behave like Olly? He had a choice: he could spend all night being scared or he could deal with this haunt as Olly would. Sitting on his bed, he said, 'All right. Let's be having you. Who or what are you and what do you want?'

There was no answer, but the cold grew deeper and took on a damp fogginess. Alex got into bed and covered himself up. 'Stop playing games,' he said. 'I know you're here.'

Something formed by the side of his bed. It was a vague, greyish blob, about four feet tall. It shifted a little, hunching itself, and seeming to sway from side to side, but didn't become any clearer.

'Is that the best you can do?' Alex asked.

'Sorry.' The word was hardly to be heard, a damp breath.

'Are you a ghost?' Alex asked.

The blob didn't really have a head, but it moved in a way that suggested it was trying to nod a head.

'Why have you come to me?' Alex asked.

'Because –' breathed the ghost. Its voice died away.

'Because? Because what?'

'I'm scared –'

Alex was too surprised to say anything. It was a new idea, that a ghost had come to him because it was scared.

'– of Olly,' the ghost breathed.

'You're scared of Olly?' It was hard to understand why anyone would be scared of Olly.

'She's so –'

'So what?' Alex said. 'So fat? So silly? So fond of motorcycle leathers and black eyeliner?'

'So alive,' breathed the ghost.

Alex thought this over. He supposed Olly was a bit – well, big. And loud. Maybe such a wispy, damp, barely-there ghost would be scared of her. He felt quite sorry for it. Poor little grey ghost. It must spend most of its time being scared of big, noisy, fully-coloured, living people. 'There's no need to be scared of Olly,' he said. 'She's really nice, really.'

'I wish . . .' sighed the ghost.

'What?'

'I wish . . .'

Alex wanted to be kind, but he was exasperated. 'You wish what?'

'I could haunt the Olde Inne,' said the grey ghost, in a rush. It shivered. 'With the others.'

'How do you know about the Inne?'

The ghost shrank, shivered.

'I'm sorry. But how do you know about the Inne?'

'I heard,' whispered the grey ghost. 'On the wind.'

'Oh,' Alex said. He supposed ghosts had their ways of finding things out. 'Well, Olly said I was to look out for another ghost.'

'Please,' whispered the ghost. 'Please ask her.'

'OK,' Alex said. 'But tomorrow, yeah? Right now, I'm going to sleep.'

He lay down, pulled the blankets over himself and closed his eyes. I'm getting quite take 'em or leave 'em about ghosts, he thought. Just like Olly.

But he couldn't sleep. The grey blob didn't do anything. It didn't bang on walls or shriek or rattle chains or any of the things that ghosts are supposed to do. It just stood by his bedside, being cold and damp and sad. The harder he tried to sleep, the colder, damper and sadder it was.

'All right!' he said, sitting up and throwing the bedclothes off. 'Honestly!' He left his bedroom and stumped down the stairs. 'Can't get a minute's peace.'

'Alex!' his mother's voice shouted, from his parents' bedroom. 'Why aren't you in bed?'

'If it's not the dead going on at you, it's the living,' Alex muttered to himself, but he shouted back, 'Just getting a drink of water, Mum! I'll be right back up.'

He didn't go into the kitchen, but the living room, switching on the light. He couldn't see the grey blob in the light, but he knew it had followed him, because the room was so cold.

In a box by the side of the computer was Olly's business card, with her email address and telephone numbers printed on it. Throwing himself down on the settee, he dialled Olly's number on the living-room phone.

It rang a long time before it was answered and then Olly's voice said, 'Blessings be!'

'Hello, Olly – it's me, Alex. Sorry to get you up –'

'Oh, I hadn't gone to bed,' Olly said. 'Just casting a spell hither and a spell yon, y'know. What's up, little pal?'

'I've got this ghost here –'

'You don't say!'

'It turned up in my bathroom – it's just a sort of grey blob.' He wanted to tell her what a poor sort of ghost it was, but he could feel it standing by him and didn't want to hurt its feelings. 'It says it wants to come to the Inne too, but it's scared to ask you.'

'You're coming on in leaps and bounds, Alex,' Olly said. 'Well, the more the merrier. Sit on it for a couple of days and then I'll heave 'em all over together.'

'Er – you might want to meet it first,' Alex said, still thinking that the grey blob wouldn't be much of an asset to the hotel.

'Nah,' Olly said. 'You keep it under your hat for the minute, that's best. Goodnight then, Al – and well done, Precious!'

She hung up, leaving Alex on the settee with the grey blob.

'You're in,' he said to it, not quite sure of where it was, but feeling its cold nearby. 'Would you mind letting me get some sleep now? I mean, when you stand by my bed, it really puts me off.'

'Sorry,' the ghost breathed. 'I'll go.'

'No, you've got to stay,' Alex said, 'or Olly won't know where to summon you from.'

'Into the garden,' whispered the ghost. 'I'll go into the garden. And watch the night.'

That seemed a boring occupation to Alex, but then the Grey Blob was boring, so maybe watching the night would make it happy. 'OK,' he said, and went off to bed.

These ghosts, he thought, as he climbed the stairs. Nothing to 'em.

7. Bring on the Ghosts!

'Are we all ready?' Olly asked. 'Here we go then. Green Lady first.'

They were gathered in one of the Olde Inne's big bedrooms. Outside, it was dark and darkness filled the long windows, with their many small, diamond-shaped panes. Inside, Olly's white candles lit the room goldenly and reflected in the glass.

It was a posh room, Alex thought, with walls painted dark red and a blue-and-white bowl of pot-pourri on the window sill, which gave out a sweet, spicy scent. Against one wall there was a big four-poster bed, with curtains. Alex was sitting on the bed, thinking that he wouldn't mind sleeping in it. Being

61

able to draw the curtains round yourself would make it cosier than an ordinary bed. It might be a bit spooky in the night, though, if you woke up and didn't know what was on the other side of the curtains. And it was very quiet, up here, in the hotel's bedrooms. The place was empty as usual, as Lisa had been complaining, and there wasn't a sound from outside the room.

'Come on, Alex,' Olly said. 'To my side, stout fellow.'

She was on the hearth, in front of a large fireplace. There were logs in the grate, as if someone might like to light a fire, even though there were radiators against the walls. Alex bounced off the bed and went over to her. She held out a hand and he took it.

'Lisa. You too.' Olly held out her other hand to her friend.

Lisa hesitated. 'Oo-er. Scary.'

'Oh, come on, don't mess about,' Olly said. 'What do you think is going to happen?'

Lisa half rose from her chair, but said, 'Well, you're going to bring a ghost here. I hope.'

'You want ghosts,' Olly said, 'you come here and help fetch 'em.'

So Lisa came across and took one of Olly's hands and one of Alex's and they stood in a small circle.

'Now, let's concentrate,' Olly said. 'Lisa, think about how much you want these ghosts to come here. Think about it until it discombobulates your brain. Want it till it hurts. Right?'

'I – er. I think so. I'll try.'

'Do better than try,' Olly said, 'or we might as well go and eat chips.'

'I'll do it,' Lisa said.

'Alex – you've seen the ghosts, so I want you to think really hard about them – about what they're like and where they're coming from. I want you to think about them so hard that you can open your eyes and see them in this room, right?'

'Er – right.'

'Green Lady first. On we go, then.' Olly gripped their hands tightly, closed her eyes and took a deep breath through her nose.

Alex shut his own eyes and started thinking about the hall at his old school. He tried to build it up in his mind. The varnished, wooden floor, all dusty, with the lines for various games painted on it, but the lines were cracking. The long windows all down one side, with curtains hanging from the ceiling to the floor. The wall at the back with the climbing frames. The stage at the other end, with the wall of bare bricks behind it.

He had just built this picture up in his mind when Olly began to chant, and almost drove it away again. He couldn't understand what she was chanting, but she said it in a deep voice and her voice swayed up and down, up and down – and the picture of the hall came into his head again and steadied and became clearer. He took a deep breath and felt a little light and giddy, as if he was swaying with the chant.

Now think about the Green Lady, he thought, and he remembered how he'd felt cold at her first coming, and he felt chilled again, from his head down, as if someone had poured cold water over him. Every little hair on his head, neck and spine tingled. Then, the

Lady had appeared, had formed herself from the shadows in a corner –

Olly was chanting more loudly –

There was a rushing sound, like a gust of wind, and Alex opened his eyes in surprise, just in time to see the Green Lady step out of the air in the middle of the room. Lisa must have opened her eyes too, because she gave a squeal, pulled her hands away from theirs and moved quickly backwards to the wall.

'It's only a ghost,' Alex said to her.

'I'm – not used to them,' Lisa said, and Alex felt quite perky and conceited at the idea that he was used to them.

Olly leaned on the mantelpiece behind her, looking as if she'd run too fast for a bus and was out of breath.

The Green Lady was looking round. 'Is this to be my new haunt?'

Since no one else seemed able to answer her, Alex did, by nodding.

'Oh, I do approve,' the Green Lady said.

She took a turn round the room, her long skirts swinging in a stately manner, as she admired the beams and the bed. 'Oh yes, much more me.' Finding herself at the foot of the big bed, she suddenly turned to face the pillows, threw back her head and gave a long scream. 'Oooooh! My sins! My unforgiven sins!' The temperature dropped sharply and the candles wavered and burned blue.

Lisa clutched at her face and tried to push herself backwards through the wall.

The Green Lady marched round the bed, rattling the curtains. She sobbed, wailed, pounded her breast and walked through the wall beside the bed's headboard.

Olly looked at Lisa, grinned and said, 'How's that?'

Lisa went to a nearby armchair and sat

down, clutching at her chest. 'I think our guests might have heart attacks.'

'They'll love it,' Olly said. 'Come on, come on. White Lady next.'

They all joined hands on the hearth again. Alex was surprised to feel that Lisa's hand was cold, damp and shaking slightly. 'Discombobulate,' Olly said, and Alex closed his eyes and started to think about the canal towpath. As Olly chanted, he was thinking about the old bridge, with its dirty bricks and moss growing in the grooves between them, about the old blue-black bricks that made the uneven path beneath it and the way sound echoed from the underside of its arch. He felt himself growing light and dizzy again and he felt as if he was hanging in the chant, as if it was holding him up – and he'd hardly even given a thought to the White Lady herself when he heard that gust of wind again and opened his eyes.

The White Lady stepped out of the air and

dripped on the carpet. Dripped was hardly the word, really. Water poured from her long white dress and from her long hair; poured and ran in puddles and rivulets over the carpet.

'Don't get your knickers in a twist about the water,' Olly said to Lisa. 'It's just your average ghostly illusion.'

The White Lady looked round. 'Indoors?' she said, folding her arms. 'What am I going to do indoors?'

'Improvise!' Olly said. 'Use the space boldly! Show some initiative.'

The White Lady hunched her shoulders in a sulky way. Water streamed down from her even faster.

'Are you sure that water isn't real?' Lisa asked.

'Put your hand in it and see,' Olly said.

Lisa drew back. 'I don't . . . No.'

'It's only a ghost,' Alex said. He was enjoying saying that.

'Is that all this one does?' Lisa asked. 'Stand there and drip?'

The White Lady looked round at her sharply.

'Very effective on a moonlit night,' said Olly.

The White Lady turned towards Lisa and raised her arms. Water cascaded from her sleeves. She drifted, floated across the carpet, as if floating in water. Her thin, clawed hands reached for Lisa, who shrank back. 'Come with me,' the White Lady said, and water spurted from her mouth. 'Leave the pains and fears of life. Come with me, under the water where it's cool and dark, come—'

'Make it stop!' Lisa said.

The White Lady laughed and stopped. 'I'll "does she only drip?" you. Haven't you got a lake? Or a pond, even? It's going to look funny, me, a water ghost, haunting a place like this. It's not even got a bit of rising damp.'

'Never mind, we can work round it,' Olly said

'It's easy,' Alex said. 'Make up a legend. Say the lady was horribly murdered in the house, but her body was chucked into – the moat. You did say there was a moat?'

'The duck pond's all that's left of it,' Lisa said.

'Well then, she was chucked into the moat and ever since then she climbs out and comes, dripping, to walk the house at dead of night. Searching for her murderer.'

Lisa seemed struck by this and was silent, thinking about it, for a moment. 'That's pretty good. We could get a pamphlet printed.'

'My little pal,' Olly said, winking at Alex. 'You could write it for them, eh, Al? For a small fee.'

'Could you make up something for the Green Lady as well?' Lisa asked, and jumped with fright as the Green Lady came sailing back through the wall, as if in answer to her name.

The Green Lady stopped short when she saw the White Lady. 'Who is this person?'

'Er – a companion for you,' Olly said. 'You might be lonely on your own.'

The Green Lady looked the White Lady up and down, her eyes shifting over the white shift – or was it a shroud? – and the constantly pouring water and dripping pond weed. 'She could only be my maid. And I couldn't have a maid who *drips*.'

The White Lady turned to Olly. Her hair whisked out and sent water flying. 'Where did you find the old hag?'

The eyes and mouth of the Green Lady rounded, but she only said, 'I need not ask where you found *her*. Do you expect me to share my haunt with *that*?'

Lisa stared at Olly, too scared to say anything herself. Alex, too, waited for Olly to sort things out.

'Send her packing, back where she come from,' the White Lady said. 'You don't need her now you got me.'

The Green Lady folded her arms and lifted her head high. 'And what kind of tone would *you* give the establishment? I know how to conduct myself in a great house.'

'Ladies, ladies!' Olly said, before the White Lady could speak again. 'There's plenty of room. You can each have your own private haunt.'

'I claim this room,' said the Green Lady. 'She had better haunt the kitchens.'

'No!' Lisa said, and everyone, ghosts and living, turned to look at her. She ducked her head, embarrassed. 'We'd never get any meals cooked,' she said.

'Tell you what,' Olly said hastily. 'Let's call along number three, shall we? Alex, you'd better –'

'There is a *third*?' the Green Lady said.

The White Lady put her hands on her hips,

and water poured from her elbows. 'How many you going to pack in here? We ain't sardines.'

'Just one more,' Olly said. 'Alex – it's your ghost, this one. You'd better call it over.'

Alex joined hands with Olly and Lisa again, feeling nervous. But the knack of concentrating seemed to become easier the more he did it. Olly chanted and he found a picture of his own house growing, pin-sharp, in his mind. And then he felt the Grey Blob coming, like a wind blowing towards him. He opened his eyes, expecting to see – her. He thought it was a her.

But the Grey Lady – the Grey Blob – didn't step into the room like the others. It hung, mistily, in a corner by the window. Olly could obviously see it, because she looked at it and smiled, as someone might at a puppy. But Lisa, looking round, said, 'Is it here?'

'Is this the best you can do?' said the Green Lady. 'Really! A soggy jezebel and a smudge?'

'A crone and a damp patch,' said the White Lady.

'Leave her alone!' Alex said, who felt responsible for the feeble Grey Blob.

The Green Lady lifted her chin, turned and swept out through the wall again. Lisa ducked her head and giggled. 'Oops! You've offended her. I shouldn't ever stay the night here, if I were you!'

'What can it do?' the White Lady demanded, staring at the Grey Blob.

'All manner and classes of things,' Olly said. 'Come on – give us a turn!'

But the Grey Blob became even fainter and disappeared. A feeling of chill, damp and despair crept through the room, but quickly faded.

'Huh!' said the White Lady. 'You'd better have that one haunting a glove-drawer – if that ain't too much for it.'

'You can talk!' Alex said. 'You can't even be dry!'

She turned on him, snaking out her neck and sticking her white, cold face into his. Icy cold, ghostly water splashed his skin. 'I'm a water ghost! Not an 'Oh-ain't-I-wonderful-I-can-walk-up-and-down-in-a-straight-line-and-scream-at-the-same-time' ghost, like *some*.' She raised her voice as she said this, but the Green Lady didn't come back.

'OK, OK,' Alex muttered, backing off. He was a bit unnerved.

'Let's be cool,' Olly said. 'Let's take time out. I've got an idea – Lise, are you still in touch with those ghost-hunters?'

'I've still got their number somewhere, yes.'

'Well, how about we have a sort of dress rehearsal? Call the ghost-hunters and invite 'em back again. Say something's disturbed the ghosts – say you've had some building work done or something –'

'We did have part of the kitchen extended last year,' Lisa said.

'Cool! Tell 'em that ever since then you've

been riddled with ghosts. That'll fetch 'em. Ghosts do shut down for a few years sometimes and then come back on line after some sort of disturbance.'

'Talk about me as if I'm not here, why don't you,' said the White Lady. 'I don't matter after all.'

'They can bring all their equipment along,' Olly went on. 'The ghosts'll put on a show. The ghost-hunters'll be thrilled and buy lots of beer and breakfasts – and we'll get on to the papers.'

'Lots of publicity!' Lisa said.

'Photos!' Olly threw herself on the bed and posed like a model, with one hand behind her head and one knee crooked. 'Olly Spellmaker, beautiful young witch – your psychic problems her speciality – in the bedroom where the ghost was seen.'

'Can I be in a photo?' Alex asked.

'Come on, then,' Olly said, and Alex jumped on the bed beside her, putting one finger under his chin and simpering. 'Olly Spellmaker, beautiful witch, and Alex, her handsome young assistant, pose in the haunted Olde Manor Inne –'

'You should be on the stage, the pair of you,' said the White Lady. 'I don't think.'

Lisa laughed and jumped up, saying, 'I'll go and find that phone number.' She ran out of the room and then came back. 'Er – will you come with me? I don't want to meet the Green Lady on my own – she was in such a miff.'

Alex and Olly went with her.

Left behind, the White Lady stood in the middle of the room and swung from side to side, spraying water from her hair and clothes. She looked over into the corner. 'You still here?' she asked. 'You'd better buck your ideas up, matey, or they'll wipe you up with a sponge and wring you out down the sink.'

8. Ghost Hunters

'Have a look at that, Alex,' Lisa said, 'and tell me what you think.' She handed him a sheet of printed paper. It turned out to be his story about the White Lady, how she'd been cruelly murdered by her wicked husband in the beautifully decorated, en-suite room now known as the 'White Lady Suite', and her body had been thrown into the moat, which could be seen from the room's window.

'Is it OK?' Lisa asked.

'Fine,' he said.

'Only it would be great if you could come up with something for the Green Lady as well. And the other one. You've got a good imagination. Better than mine.'

'I'll think about it,' Alex said.

'And then I could get it all printed. I'm glad your mum and dad let you come. I didn't think they would, for an all-night thing like this.'

'They weren't very happy about it,' Alex said. 'But Olly talked to them. Told 'em it was educational. And character-building. And mind-broadening. I don't think they were convinced, really. I think they agreed just so she'd stop.'

'I'm glad you're here, anyway,' Lisa said. 'What with Olly and this lot, I need somebody sane around.'

'This lot' were the ghost-hunters. There were six of them, and they'd brought with them thermometers, cameras, tape recorders, video cameras, bags of flour, rolls of sellotape and reels of cotton, all of which they'd stacked on their table in the bar.

'The old ways are the best,' Keith McBride had told them. 'None of these new-fangled gimmicks and gadgets for us.' He was the big man who seemed to be the ghost-hunter's leader. He was very tall – he had to duck through every door in the Inne - and very fat, and had a lot of red hair and a big red beard. In amongst the hair, he wore spectacles with thick dark frames. He had on jeans and trainers and an enormous woolly jacket with a big, bright plaid pattern, mostly red, and cuffs and a collar of grubby sheepskin. When he got hot and took it off, he had a green corduroy shirt on underneath, with ink stains round its pocket. 'Some people these days spend thousands on machines to measure electro-magnetism and whatnot, but where's the point of that? You can get just as much evidence of a ghost with the basics. Flour on the floor – if it's a ghost, it won't make footprints. Cotton across doorways – '

''Cos if it's a ghost, it won't break it,' Alex said.

'Bright lad! And then we've got the cameras

to record any odd visual manifestations, and the tape recorders – '

'A video camera'll record sound,' Alex said. 'So why do you want tape recorders as well?'

'A very bright lad,' McBride said, looking approvingly at Lisa and Olly. 'But think about it. You need somebody to operate a video camera. But you can leave a tape recorder running on its own in an empty room.'

'Ah,' Alex said. 'And then go back and see what's recorded. I expect you've seen loads of ghosts.'

'I should say we have,' said Mrs McBride. She was much shorter than her husband, but also rather round and fat. When she'd first come in, she'd had on a dark anorak with the hood drawn tightly round her face so that you could only see her chin, her nose, and her glasses, which were dark and thick-framed, like her husband's. When she took the anorak off, she had on jeans and a warm, woolly, hooded fleece in a vivid snot-green. 'We've got albums full of photos and bookshelves full of notes.'

'Aha, yes,' said Mr McBride, and took a reporter's notebook from his pocket. He waved it at them. 'Because this – this – is the most important tool the ghost-hunter has. The notebook! Everything to be written down! Times noted, temperatures, sounds heard, everything!'

There was a girl with them, and she took a notebook from her pocket. 'I've got mine!' She actually jumped up and down. 'I can't wait to get started!' She was about eighteen. Her name was Beth. There was a young man named Shaun, who kept close beside her. Alex thought he looked bored. He was probably only there because Beth was.

The other two ghost-hunters were a tall, thin man named Clive, and another man with a beard and glasses named Doug. He had dark hair, though, and not nearly so much of it as McBride. In fact, he was going bald on top.

'The first thing we have to do – and this is vitally important,' said McBride, 'is to have a drink and something to eat.'

His ghost-hunters cheered, and Lisa was pleased, as it meant some money in the till. Olly and Alex sat down with the ghost-hunters and Olly treated Alex to fish fingers and chips, while she had the spicy sausage, and after everyone had finished eating, she demonstrated how to throw peanuts in the air and catch them in your mouth. Mr McBride and Shaun had a go, but neither of them were as good as Olly. Neither of them had waggling skeleton earrings, for a start.

'Right!' Mr McBride said. 'The second vitally important thing is for us to have a recce of the place and make a sketch map. Note all the rooms.'

'Didn't you do that last time you were here?' Alex asked.

'Bright lad,' said Mr McBride. 'But you see, Alex, it's important that we reacquaint ourselves with the layout again – and Beth and Shaun weren't here the last time.'

'And there might have been alterations,' Doug said. 'Something's made the ghosts active again.'

'Yes, yes,' McBride agreed. 'Lisa, didn't you say – ?'

'We had the kitchen made larger,' Lisa said. 'I'll give you a tour.'

'Have you noticed if any particular areas of the building are particularly active?' Mrs McBride asked. Her round face was rather flushed now, and her short dark hair bushed out in all directions.

'Active?' Lisa asked. Alex almost laughed – he had a quick vision of the hotel doing push-ups.

'Do the phenomena materialize in any particular place more than others?'

'She means,' Alex said, 'where have you seen ghosts? In what rooms?'

'Or heard them,' Mrs McBride said.

'Or smelled them,' said her husband.

Olly stooped down and whispered in Alex's ear, 'Ghostly farts!' They both giggled, while trying to hide it.

'I didn't know you could smell ghosts,' Lisa said.

'Oh yes, yes,' said Mr McBride. 'Perfume or wood-smoke – I've known a bit of BO before now!'

'They should use their *Life*guard deodorant,' Olly whispered, and she and Alex giggled again. It wasn't that the jokes were really funny – but they seemed it at the time.

Then they'd all left the bar, going first to the kitchens and then climbing the back stairs to troop round the upper part of the hotel, crowding each other in doorways and on stairs. The place seemed anything but ghostly with so many tramping boots and voices. When they reached the room with the four-poster, where Olly and Alex had called the ghosts through, Olly piped up. 'I think I remember you saying, Lise, that a ghost had been seen in *this* room?'

'Oh – yes!' Lisa said.

'A green lady, wasn't it?' Alex chimed in.

'Oh – I think it was.'

'Well, certainly we should have someone posted in this room, then,' said Mrs McBride. 'Who's it going to be?'

'Me! Me!' Beth said, but Mr McBride said, 'I think we ought to look round the rest before we decide on that. Agreed?'

Lisa led the way along the corridor to the other rooms and Alex fell back with Olly. 'Where is the White Lady going to be?'

'That room at the end, overlooking the bit of moat,' Olly said. 'And then the little room across from it, that's where your Grey Blob is going to strut her stuff.'

'Don't you call her a blob,' Alex said. 'You should have a bit of respect, at least.' He was fed up with the way everyone sneered at the ghost he'd recruited.

'Sor-ree!'

The ghost-hunters looked into the other two haunted rooms, and stood in a bunch at the end of the landing, drawing their sketch maps in their notebooks and discussing who should go where.

'I gather that the Green Lady and the White Lady are the most active,' Mr McBride said.

'So we should have our most experienced team members in those rooms.'

Beth groaned. 'I want to see a ghost!'

'How about I watch for the Grey Lady by myself?' Doug said. 'She's the least active, so probably there'll be nothing to record. Then Beth and Shaun can be split between the other teams and have a chance to experience something.'

Beth grinned and looked excited. Shaun looked bored.

'Good, good,' Mr McBride said. 'Right, Beth with me and Ellie in the Green Lady's room –' Beth danced and cheered. 'And Shaun with Clive in the White Lady's room.' Shaun looked annoyed, but didn't say anything. 'Right, shall we fetch our gear and set up? And Beth, Shaun,' he added, as they walked back towards the stairs. 'Remember. Never whisper. Always talk normally. Then nothing you say can be confused with phenomena. OK?'

Olly and Alex helped the group carry all their gear up to the landing, where they started to unzip bags. Mr McBride took out a clipboard, with a checklist. 'Doug – you're by yourself in the Grey Lady's room. Right – torch?'

'Check,' Doug said, taking a torch out of his bag and waving it.

'Spare batteries?'

'Check.'

'Still camera?'

'Check.'

'Flashes?'

'Check.'

'Thermometers?'

'Check, two.'

'Tape recorder?'

'Check.'

'Flour?'

'Check.'

'Cotton and sellotape?'

'Check, check.'

'Notebook and pens?'

'Check, check.'

'Right, you're sorted. Now, Clive and Shaun, you're in the White Lady's room –' And they went through a similar checklist, except that this one included a video camera and spare tapes. Finally, Mr and Mrs McBride checked through their own equipment.

'What about our two observers?' Clive asked. He meant Olly and Alex.

Mrs McBride smiled at them. 'Would you like to choose which group to join?'

'We'd prefer to be nomadic observers,' Olly said. 'Wandering from room to room, bringing cheer, encouragement, hot tea and choccie biccies.'

'Oh, that sounds good!' Mrs McBride said.

'Well . . . so long as you remember always to speak in a normal voice,' said Mr McBride. 'And announce yourself as you come into a room, so there's no confusion about the sound of the door opening.'

'We'll remember,' Alex said.

'Right. Synchronize watches.'

Most people agreed that it was ten minutes past eleven, and everyone else had to alter their watches to that. Alex was surprised to hear it was so late. He wasn't feeling tired. Too excited, he supposed.

The ghost-hunters all tramped off to their separate rooms with their bags of equipment, leaving Alex and Olly on the landing. Olly looked at her watch. 'The Green Lady's due to show at dead on midnight. Shall we see if Lise can do us some hot chocolate?'

They spent the time they had to wait drinking hot chocolate with marshmallows in the bar. There were a couple of other customers, but nothing like a crowd. Lisa, joining them, said, 'I hope this works. I'm losing money hand over fist.'

'Ten to twelve,' Olly said. 'The very witching time of night, when fairies strike and graves give up their dead. Shall we go up? After you.' She made a sweeping bow to usher Alex from the bar.

'No. After you.'

'After you.'

They after-you'd each other out of the bar and up the stairs. In the upper corridor, it was hushed and dark. They knew there were people in the rooms, but you would never have guessed it.

Olly opened the door of the 'Green Lady's Chamber' and walked in, saying, 'Only us!'

'Hello!' said Mrs McBride, who was lying on the bed. 'Did you bring those biccies?'

'Sorry, no. Anything happened?'

Mrs McBride yawned. 'Not a dicky bird. We've got some biccies, if you want some, but they're only ginger nuts.'

'There's plenty of time yet, though!' Beth said. She had a notebook in one hand and a pen in the other, ready for anything that might happen.

'Hello!' Mr McBride said. He was standing by one of the bedposts, where he'd tied a thermometer. 'The temperature's dropping like a stone.'

'"Twelve midnight",' Beth scribbled. '"Temperature dropping like stone". What to?'

'Anybody feel it?' Mr McBride asked, looking round.

Alex could. The skin of his arms, beneath his shirt and jumper, was goose-pimpling. Before anyone else could speak, the room was cut through by a scream that drilled into their ears and made Mrs McBride jerk upright on the bed.

Through the wall beside the bed came the Green Lady, her arms raised, her fists clenched. She screamed again, a scream that seemed to drive hooks into the heart and drag them out again. Alex felt the blood drain from his face, even though he knew the Green Lady and the way she carried on. You just couldn't hear that scream and be unaffected.

Beth, he saw, had dropped her pen and notebook. Mr McBride was standing by the bedpost, his mouth hanging open.

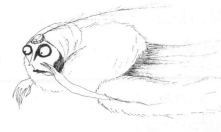

The Green Lady seemed disconcerted to find him standing at the foot of the bed and stopped short. 'Oh, my uncon—'she started but then, as she turned to face the room, there they all were, staring at her. Mrs McBride on the bed, Mr McBride at the foot of it, Beth on its other side, with both her hands at her face, and Olly and Alex by the door. 'Oh, my—' the Green Lady started again, but feebly. 'Oh!' she said, and vanished.

'Well!' said Mrs McBride, and bit into a ginger nut. 'Short but sweet.'

Mr McBride took his own notebook from his pocket and wrote intently. Beth said, her voice shaking, 'Was that a *real* ghost?'

Mr McBride looked up and looked round at them all. 'I take it we all saw it, then?'

'Oh, yes,' said his wife. 'Do you think that's it for tonight?'

'We saw it,' Olly said and Alex nodded.

'A real ghost,' Beth said. 'I saw a real ghost.' She didn't sound happy about it, somehow.

'Come and have a biscuit, love,' Mrs McBride said. 'Your first one's always a bit of a shock.'

Beth crept across to the bed. Olly nodded to Alex, and they tiptoed out on to the landing.

'What was all that about?' Olly said. 'Big screams. Lots of wellie. Then, "Oh my!" And that's your lot.'

'The ghost-hunters didn't seem to mind,' Alex said.

'They aren't paying punters,' Olly said, 'coughing up for bed, breakfast, and the ghostly experience of a lifetime. I think they'll want a bit more for their money than a couple of screams.'

'They were *good* screams,' Alex said. 'She'll do better next time. It was stage fright. I remember when I was playing a shepherd, and I had to come on and say, "Here is where the star has led us". I was fine until the first night, when I came on, and suddenly there were all these strangers staring at me. And I just stood there. Didn't say anything. Stage fright. I don't suppose you've ever had it.'

'Not that I remember,' Olly said. 'And I didn't know you could get it when you're dead. Well, let's go and catch the twelve-thirty.' She led the way along the landing to the room where Clive and Shaun were waiting for the White Lady. Opening the door, she asked, 'Everything hunky-dory and peachy-keen?'

It was a less grand room than the Green Lady's chamber, with two neat modern beds. Shaun was sprawled in an armchair with his hands in his pockets, looking at the ceiling, very fed up. Clive was sitting on the bed with his notebook next to him. 'All quiet,' he said. 'Have the others had any luck, d'you know?'

'Oh, they think they might have heard something,' Olly said. 'Cheer up, Shaun – it'll never happen.'

Shaun shifted in his chair, sighed, and looked even more fed up.

Olly sat down by Clive and started chatting – they quickly found out that they both liked motorbikes and Olly told the tale of how hers was off the road and Clive told her about all the troubles he'd had with one he used to own. Alex was getting almost as bored as Shaun by the time the White Lady appeared.

The temperature dropped, as before. Alex noticed it and started rubbing his arms, but Shaun was too bored and Clive and Olly too deep in their talk about motorbikes.

Then Alex saw the curtains moving, as if in a strong breeze. He said, 'Er –' and pointed.

Clive looked round, saw the curtains billow and grabbed the video camera from the bedside table. He jumped up and started filming the curtains.

Through the curtains, with arms outstretched, came the White Lady. Water poured from her. She opened her mouth and water spouted from it. A nasty smell of dank, green ponds filled the room. All very nice touches, Alex thought. She was doing very well.

Shaun had shot upright in his chair and was

staring, bored no longer. The White Lady stretched her arms towards him, water cascading from her sleeves. Shaun went as white as her dress. He looked as if he was going to leap up and run. 'Come, come with me –' the White Lady crooned.

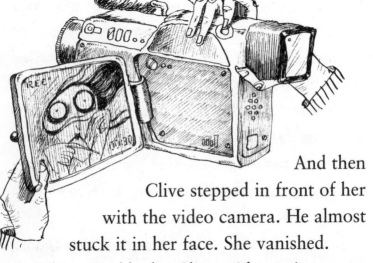

And then Clive stepped in front of her with the video camera. He almost stuck it in her face. She vanished.

'Oh . . . Bad luck!' Clive said, turning away. 'Sometimes these appearances don't last very long.'

You fool! Alex wanted to shout. If you'd given her a bit of space – !

Shaun stood still. He was pointing at the place where the Lady had been and gibbering. Just gibbering. Alex listened with interest.

'Time?' Clive said. He'd put down the camera and picked up his pen and notepad. 'Oh-Oh-twenty-five. Now let me check the temperature.' He bent over and peered at a thermometer on a bedside table.

Alex and Olly looked at each other, raised their brows, and crept out. 'Only the Grey Blob now,' Olly said. 'I don't suppose she'll show up at all.'

'Don't suppose so,' Alex agreed. But they crossed the corridor and went into the 'Grey Lady's Chamber' anyway.

It was a smaller room than the others, with only a single bed, and it was dimly lit by the bedside lamp. Doug was sitting comfortably in an armchair, reading a book. He looked up when they came in.

'I am the ghost of Auntie Mabel,' Olly said,

in a quavery voice, 'and that pound note stays on the table!'

Doug laughed, and said, 'I am the ghost of Davy Crockett, and that pound note goes in my pocket!' They both laughed. Alex thought they were cracked. 'Seen the others?' Doug asked. 'Anything happened?'

'Nothing much,' Olly said. 'How about you?'

'Nothing. 'Mind you, we draw a blank more often than we record anything at all. That's the nature of the game.'

Olly threw herself down on the bed and Alex went and sat beside her. If the ghost-hunters had scared the Green Lady and the White Lady, he thought, they would terrify the poor little Grey Blob – and, at the best of times, she was hardly noticeable.

Doug gave a big yawn and stretched his long arms. 'I wished I'd stayed at home. I'd be in bed, asleep, by now.' With his arms still crooked in the air, he said, 'What's that?'

'What?' Olly asked.

'Listen!'

They listened. There was a scratching sound, a soft thumping. It came from the door. 'It's a cat!' Alex said. 'There's a cat outside.' He jumped off the bed and opened the door. No cat came in.

He looked out into the corridor. There was no cat. Yet the sound – like a cat padding with its paws at the base of the door – had gone on even when his hand had been on the door handle.

'Nothing there. . .' he said to Doug and Olly.

From the corner of the room, behind Doug's armchair, came a low, wicked laugh.

Doug leaped up from his chair and spun round to face the corner. Even Olly sat up on the bed.

There was nothing to be seen.

9. The Grey Blob

Doug laughed himself, rather nervously. 'I'm glad I've got the tape recorder running.'

Instantly there came the clacking sound of a button being pressed and then the whizzing sound of tape rewinding. They all looked at each other and then Doug jumped to the little table where he'd placed the tape recorder. Pressing a button, he stopped it, then picked it up and examined it. 'The tape wasn't finished,' he said. 'It didn't rewind by itself. And none of us were anywhere near it. You saw that, didn't you?'

'Ye-e-s,' Olly said, sounding puzzled.

Alex didn't like being by himself, near the door. He wanted to go and sit by Olly, but he didn't like to close the door and shut them in the room with whatever had laughed so nastily in the corner. He left the door half open and went to the bed.

Doug went back to the armchair, picked up his notebook from the floor and made notes. 'Seems to have gone quiet.' Taking the tape recorder from the table, he sat in his chair again and switched the recorder to play. He kept stopping and starting it, until he found the place where they heard the button click again and the recording stop. He put it on the floor at his feet and switched it to record once more. 'Interesting. I hope the others are getting something as good as this.'

Alex sniffed the air.

'What's up?' Olly asked. 'You smell something?'

Alex sniffed again. 'Is it that po-poori stuff? No. It's –'

Olly sniffed. 'Lavender. Can you smell it, Doug?'

'Yes! You're not wearing perfume, are you?'

'Me?' Olly said. 'I never wear perfume.'

The room was filling with a strong scent of lavender – so strong that it made Alex feel a bit sick. And then a voice whispered – a loud whisper, and one that felt like fingers stroking at the back of Alex's neck, 'Here I am again.'

Alex's heart started to thump. He turned his head, looking all round, into all the corners. The others were too. From the corner of his eye Alex saw something move – he thought it was the swish of a long skirt – and he jumped up and stared. But there was no one where he'd seen the movement. He looked round and saw that Doug was on his feet too, staring in another direction. 'Did you see it?' Doug asked.

'See what?' Alex and Olly asked almost together.

'I thought I saw someone – over there.' He pointed into the far corner, by the table. No one was there.

In the opposite corner, behind the bed – behind Olly – someone laughed again. This time it sounded like a woman, and it was a snigger: an unkind, jeering snigger.

Olly jumped off the bed and joined Doug in the middle of the room. Alex pressed close to both of them.

At the foot of the bed, the familiar misty grey smudge appeared. It grew upward, changed its shape, became more solid, and there, standing in front of them, was a tall, beautiful, young woman. She wore a long, grey gown and a grey bonnet with a wide peak that framed her face as she gazed at them with large grey eyes, and smiled. As they looked at her, the face inside the bonnet vanished. They were looking at a body, with hands folded in front of its gown, but no head inside its bonnet.

As they watched, unable to speak or move, the body hunched. It twisted, melted to mist again and reformed, and this time it was an old, old woman, who leered at them from the corner of her eyes, with her head turned sideways. Her chin turned up to meet her nose, which turned down; her mouth grimaced, her eyes were red; and her big-knuckled, veined hands twisted and worked just under her chin. 'Here I am again!' she said, and laughed – it was the wicked laugh they'd heard from the corner behind the chair. Before the laughter finished, she'd vanished.

'Blimey!' Doug said, and grabbed for his notebook again.

Alex pulled at Olly's sleeve and pointed.

Seated in the armchair was the beautiful, young woman in the grey dress – the Grey Lady. When they looked at her, she smiled and said, 'No one is going to *sleep* in *this* room!' She faded away, taking the scent of lavender with her.

'You can say that again!' Olly said, and looked at Alex. 'Want to stay for more or shall we go?'

'Let's go,' Alex said. He'd thought he'd grown used to ghosts, but the Grey Lady had shaken him. Especially as – well, who would have thought the little grey blob could put on such a show?

10. A Night-time Visitation

The photograph in the newspaper showed the ghost-hunters gathered together, holding their video cameras and bags of flour, outside the entrance to the Olde Manor Inne. 'Screams in the night . . .' said the caption underneath and the short article mentioned the exciting goings-on at this fine, seven-hundred-year-old hotel and former manor house.

Alex put the clipping down on his bedside table and turned over, feeling that he had done his fair share of good deeds for the next month or so. Lisa's business would soon be booming, and Olly's bike would be back on the road . . .

'Wha'?' Alex said. 'Go away.'

A police siren, an ambulance shriek, sliced through a blurry dream of chasing his Maths teacher with a whirring hedgecutter.

'Oh my sins!' screamed the teacher. 'Oh my unconfessed and unforgiven sins!'

That didn't seem right, even for Mrs Witty. Alex woke up.

Standing by his bed, gently glimmering in the darkness, was not only the Green Lady, but the White Lady too, both of them shrieking.

Before he could ask what they were doing there, he heard his mother calling his name, and his father's deeper voice asking what was going on. Then his mother, Kirsty, burst in, wearing the old T-shirt she slept in, and with her hair all on end. Behind her was his father, Rob, in his boxer shorts and black socks.

It was hard to tell who was the more startled, his parents or the ghosts. When she saw the White and Green Ladies, Kirsty leaped back with a yell, colliding with Rob and almost knocking him down.

'What the hell – ?' Rob demanded.

The White Lady vanished, which made Kirsty shriek again. The Green Lady did what she always did – gave a blood-freezing, paralysing scream.

Kirsty yelled, 'Help! Police! Fire!'

The Green Lady screamed back. Rob put his hands over his ears. The White Lady reappeared and Kirsty gave another frightened yell.

Alex saw the Green Lady open her

mouth and leaped out of bed. 'Shut up! Shut up! Mum – Dad – they're only ghosts!'

'I thought we'd got rid of ghosts,' Rob said.

'I want no ghosts in this house!' Kirsty shouted. 'I've had my bellyful of ghosts!'

'Oh my sins – !' the Green Lady began.

'Shut up!' Alex yelled. 'Listen. Mum, Dad – go back to bed, and I'll deal with this.'

'Don't you dare move any more ghosts in,' Kirsty said.

'They won't be moving in,' Alex said. 'I promise. Go back to bed. I'll sort it out.'

His mother didn't look at all convinced or happy. 'You'd better.' She went back on to the landing.

'And keep the noise down,' Rob said. 'We've all got to get up tomorrow.'

Once his parents had gone back to their room, Alex looked at the two ghosts standing by his bed. The Green Lady was holding herself very upright and dignified; the White Lady was dripping. Both looked, he thought, even more harassed and gaunt and haggard than ever.

'What's all the screaming about?' he asked. 'And how did you get here?'

'With a lot of trouble,' said the White Lady, folding her arms. 'This travelling about isn't as easy as Olly let on.'

'But we had to find you,' said Green. 'We had to wake you. So we screamed.'

'I should think you've woken half the street! What do you want?'

'We can't be doing with it,' said the White Lady.

'With what?'

'That thing,' said White.

'That creature,' said Green.

'What are you talking about?'

'That thing of yours,' White said.

Alex was baffled.

Green raised her hands as if she was about to scream. 'That – that – '

'That *smudge*,' said White.

'It calls itself the Grey Lady, but it's no lady.'

'It's not even a ghost, not what you'd call a ghost,' said White.

Alex realized they were talking about the Grey Blob. 'What's it done?'

'Done? *Done?*' cried Green, her voice rising towards another shriek.

'Sssh,' Alex begged.

'What hasn't it done?' White said. 'It wants rid of us.'

'I don't know what you're talking about,' Alex said. 'Why come and bother me and not Olly? *She*'s the witch.'

'Precisely,' said Green. 'She's a witch.'

'We can't get near that one,' White explained. 'Trust her to look after herself.'

'She's too skilful a witch,' said Green. 'She guards herself. She can talk with us when she pleases, but we can't get near her if she doesn't want us.'

Alex realized something else, something

which made him feel a little foolish. That was why the Grey Blob had come to him. Not because it was scared of Olly, but because it couldn't reach her.

'But you,' said White. 'You don't know A from a bull's foot. Any old clabbernapper or wirrikow could get through to you.'

'Thanks a lot,' Alex said.

'You've a lot to learn, chummy.' White folded her arms, and water poured from her elbows to the floor.

'Yes, all right, all right – but I still don't know what the Grey – the Grey Lady's supposed to have done.'

'Run us out of house and haunt,' said White.

'Haunted *us*,' said Green. 'It had the gall to haunt us.'

'How?' Alex said.

'It never gave us a moment's peace all day long,' Green said. 'Screamed in our ears, pulled our hair –'

'Tried to dry me out with a hairdryer,' White said.

'Came as a priest to hear my confession,' said Green.

'Put frogs on me to "make me more at home".'

'Came as policeman to ask me about my crimes.'

'It's no ghost – it's a shapeshifter,' said White. 'You never knew what it would turn up as next.'

'And now where can I go?' Green asked. 'I left my old home. I'm a ghost without a haunt.'

'I don't want to go back to that dirty old canal,' said White.

Downstairs, the phone rang.

'It's the Grey Thing!' Green cried. 'It's after us!'

From the bedroom next door came Kirsty's shout. 'What now? It's the neighbours, ringing about the noise!'

'I'll get it,' Alex shouted back, and ran downstairs.

He went to the telephone in the hall, near the front door. As he lifted the receiver, White and Green appeared on either side of him. White was halfway through the hall's wall. 'Hello?' he said.

'Is that Alex?' It was a woman's voice, sounding panicky.

'Who's this?' Alex asked. The voice was familiar, but he couldn't quite remember where he'd heard it.

'Lisa! You know – from the Olde Manor Inne – Oh!' Something had startled her. In the background were crashes and bangs.

'What's up?' Alex asked.

'Do you know where Olly is? Can you get in touch with her?'

'I dunno. At home in bed, I suppose.'

'I've rung, I've emailed, I can't –' There was another crash, and something like a roar, a lion's roar. Lisa said, her voice rising, 'I've *got* to find Olly, Alex.'

'I don't –' Alex said. 'I'll try –'

The doorbell rang.

Upstairs, Kirsty yelled, 'What now?'

Alex was standing by the door and he opened it. On the step stood Olly.

11. Fire!

'Olly!' Alex said, and held the receiver towards her. 'Lisa's on the phone. She's been trying to find you.'

Olly came in as Kirsty came to the top of the stairs. Taking the receiver, Olly said, 'Watcha, Lise!'

'Olly,' Kirsty shouted. 'Just what's going on? There are ghosts of yours here and –'

'Mum, not now,' Alex said.

'Don't tell *me*, "not now".' Kirsty came down the stairs.

'Oh, sure,' Olly was saying into the phone. 'Too right. With the speed of light, my old chuckie flower.'

As Kirsty reached the bottom of the stairs, Olly put the phone down and said, 'Shovel some clothes on, Al, me old pal. We've got things to do.'

'Just a moment,' Kirsty said. 'He's not going anywhere with you in the middle of the night.'

'Lisa's in big trouble,' Olly said.

'Due to you, no doubt,' Kirsty said.

Alex squeezed past her to the stairs, said, 'I'll be right down,' and ran up them.

'Did I speak?' Kirsty demanded. 'What did I just say? Tell me!'

'Oh, not now, Mum,' Alex called, as he disappeared on to the landing.

'He needs his sleep,' Kirsty said, facing Olly. 'He's not going anywhere but back to bed.'

'I really need him, Kirsty,' Olly said. 'Can't manage without him.'

'You'll have to,' Kirsty said. 'Rob! Rob, come down here.'

Alex came down instead, in jeans and a jumper. He ran straight through White and

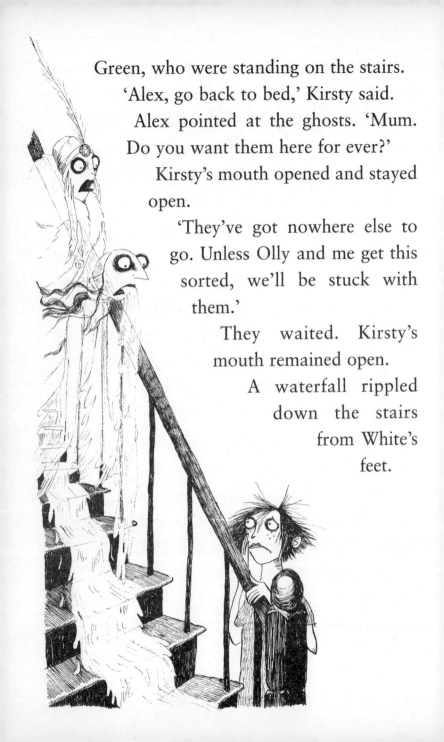

Green, who were standing on the stairs.

'Alex, go back to bed,' Kirsty said.

Alex pointed at the ghosts. 'Mum. Do you want them here for ever?'

Kirsty's mouth opened and stayed open.

'They've got nowhere else to go. Unless Olly and me get this sorted, we'll be stuck with them.'

They waited. Kirsty's mouth remained open.

A waterfall rippled down the stairs from White's feet.

'Oh, my unconfessed sins,' said Green, with a small, but piercing scream.

'Oh – go!' Kirsty said. 'But this is the last time!'

Alex and Olly ducked out of the house fast. As they went down the dark path to where the little Nova waited under a streetlight, Olly said, 'Pretty fine, pal. Couldn't have persuaded her better myself.'

It was so late – or so early, Alex wasn't sure which – that even the roads in the centre of town were empty. Once they were outside the town, everything was silent and deserted. There was plenty of time to talk.

'They say the Grey Blob isn't a ghost,' Alex said, puzzled.

'I had my suspicions when it put on that five-star performance for the ghost-hunters,' Olly said. 'It just wasn't like a ghost to be that inventive. They usually stick to their old routine.'

'Oh, my unconfessed sins,' Alex said.

'On the nail, little pal. I should have guessed when the Grey Blob came to you. It probably knew that if it came straight to me, I should spot it for what it was. Still, I should have known better. If I hadn't been so keen to get these ghosts together, and get Stormrider back on the road, I should have been more careful and checked up on it.'

'But what is it?' Alex asked.

'I think it's what us witches call a brag. Well, some of us call 'em kows, spelt with a "K". Witches never can agree. Or spell.'

'So! What's a brag? Or a kow?

'Well . . . A lubber-fiend. Or a petty-fiend. Sort of like a poltergeist – but a bit different.'

Alex sighed.

'They're like pucks and poukas – sort of practical jokers. A bit wild, a bit wicked, won't play by the rules. They can be a bit dangerous, but they aren't, usually. They play a bit rough, though. Not the sort of thing you want haunting a respectable hotel. Lise will want her money back.' Olly sighed too. 'Sometimes I'm just slapdash.'

'I'm sorry,' Alex said.

'Not your fault, little pal. How were you to know? No. It was my job. I should have checked.

They reached the sign for the Inne, and turned into the long drive. As they rounded the last bend and came in sight of the old building, Alex cried out in horror. It was on fire.

12. A Brag

Flames rose high from the hotel's roof, bursting from the windows, crackling and roaring.

'Be cool,' Olly said. 'It's not real. It's just the brag.'

'There's fire everywhere!'

'If it was real, we'd have seen the glow in the sky from miles away. And if it was real and this far on, we'd be up to our ears in fire engines. Trust me. It's the brag.'

They got out of the car. The flames roared, crackled, flashed and reflected in the windscreen and bonnet – and then they weren't there. Everything was suddenly very quiet, and the Inne was just as usual: old, solid, lit spookily by blueish floodlights.

Before they could reach the door, Lisa came running out. 'Oh thank the Lord! Everybody's gone – run away! I'm all on my own with it!'

From inside the hotel came a raucous sound, like a donkey with hiccups, laughing.

Olly looked at Alex. 'Forward, *mon brave*!' she said, and led the way into the hotel. Alex, who wasn't feeling at all brave, followed. Brags usually didn't hurt people, Olly had said. What if this was an unusual brag?

Down the stairs, clattering, banging and hee-hawing came a –

Well, it was something like a donkey. An exuberant, cartoonist's idea of a something like a donkey, except that it was real and running about in front of them.

It was bigger than a donkey, for a start, as big as a horse. It had enormous ears that wagged and flicked; and enormous eyes that rolled and winked; and enormous teeth, all showing in a big grin.

Its legs were long, bony, and shot off in all

directions. On the ends of them it had big paws, like a dog – but it still made a deafening noise on the wooden floorboards, as if it had hooves.

Behind it, held high in the air, was a tail with a stiff, splayed tuft on the end. The whole beast was striped, like a zebra. And it was blue.

It laughed and hee-hawed as it charged down the stairs, skidded on the floor at the bottom as it turned a corner with its legs kicking out to the sides and then it ran, braying with loud, manic laughter, away down the corridor, its paws clumping and clopping. As it vanished round the corner at the end of the corridor, its laughter became more wild and taunting. It was obviously having a whale of a time.

'Blimey!' Alex said.

No one else had time to say anything before the brag came charging down the stairs again, even more spiky and leggy, laughing even more loudly – only this time it was purple and spotty. Once more it racketed away down the corridor and disappeared round the corner with a whoop.

Then it came back the other way and rushed up the stairs. They listened to it clattering and crashing along the landing.

'It's been doing that for *hours*,' Lisa said.

'Oh bless. Poor sausage,' said Olly.

Lisa pushed her hair about with her hands. 'We actually had some guests. A couple of New Zealanders. They'd seen the local paper and the thing about the

ghost-hunt, and they'd come and found us out, 'cos they'd always wanted to stay in an old haunted inn in England. So it was working! The ghosts were getting us custom. And they loved the place. They were going to stay at least two nights – and then this thing started up. It wasn't an hour before they packed up and left.'

'Wusses,' Alex said. 'They wanted a haunted house.'

'They wanted a nice, normal ghost,' Lisa said. 'Something that would appear for ten minutes, let them get some sleep, and give them something to tell their friends about. Not *this*.'

'It's gone ever so quiet,' Olly said, looking around.

'Oh no. That means it's thinking up something new. Olly – get rid of it!'

'Let's be cool,' Olly said. 'Let's go and sit down and you can pour out your heart to Auntie Olly.'

'We could go and sit in the car,' Lisa said. She looked scared and obviously didn't want to stay in the hotel at all.

'Never show fear,' Olly said. 'It only encourages them.' She led the way into the Inne's bar, with Alex and Lisa following her closely.

All the lights were on and so the thick blood that dripped from the ceiling to form a widening pool on the floor looked very red and shiny.

'That's another thing it keeps doing,' Lisa said. 'It's not hygienic.'

Olly walked straight through the falling blood. It seemed to engulf her like a shower, but when she walked out on the other side, she hadn't a drop on her, nor did she leave bloody footprints. 'It's not real,' she said, over her shoulder.

'No,' Lisa said, walking round the pool, 'but people think it is, and they don't like it. Especially when they're eating.'

Alex would have liked to have walked through the blood, but at the last moment he didn't quite have the nerve and swerved aside. It looked so real and sticky.

They joined Olly at a table, just as a green giant, with a ball and chain on his leg, stumped through the bar, heaving the ball along and carrying his toothy, grinning head by the hair.

'It was something like that it scared the kitchen staff away with,' Lisa said, watching the giant as it crossed the room and left by an opposite door. It ducked, even though it had no head on its neck to bump. 'Only it had a cleaver through the head. And took it out and waved it about.'

'Dripping blood?' Olly asked.

'Spraying blood.'

'They have a sense of humour all their own,' Olly said.

Lisa looked cross. 'I'm not laughing!'

The green giant ducked back into the room

and started playing throw up and catch with his head, but he must have become bored with that, because he melted into the donkey thing – bright orange this time – and galloped noisily about, nickering, hee-hawing and laughing.

'Olly!' Lisa had her fingers in her ears. 'Can you get rid of it? I want the White and Green Ladies back! I was doing well with them!'

Olly slid out from behind the table, stood, moved into the middle of the room, drew herself up as tall as she could, and tried to look impressive. Alex wanted to giggle, as he didn't think Olly could look impressive, not even in her motorbike leathers.

In a deep, commanding voice, Olly said, 'Petty-fiend, I command you, in the name of the Goddess whom I serve, to leave this place and never return.'

The din of galloping stopped. The silence was deep. Nothing happened for a long moment and Alex held his breath. Was a simple order all it took to banish a brag?

Something moved near Olly's feet. They all stared at it. A large, naked green bum, as big as an armchair, rose through the floor. It remained still for a moment, before their surprised eyes, in all its large, green, naked bumness. Then it farted, and sank out of sight.

Alex laughed and laughed. He laughed so much, he slipped off the bench and lay on the floor.

'I take it that's our answer,' Olly said. 'Such eloquence!'

Lisa stood and shouted, 'Get rid of it! Olly, if you want the rest of your money, get rid of it!'

'All *right*,' Olly said. 'All right. Keep *your* knickers on at least.'

Alex, who had just managed to stop laughing, collapsed again.

13. A Coffee Jar

'This time, it's personal,' Olly said. 'This time, we chant it down.'

'We what?' Alex asked.

'We chant it down.'

Lisa was hugging herself nervously and looking all around in case the brag made another appearance.

'How do we do that?' Alex asked.

'It's easy enough to do,' Olly said, 'but it takes a lot of concentration. Especially if a brag is frolicking about your ears while you're doing it. Gone quiet, hasn't it?'

'It's thinking up something new,' Lisa said.

'I think my commanding it to be gone gave it a bit of a shock,' Olly said. 'But you're right. It'll be back. So. First we invoke the Goddess.'

'How?' Alex asked.

'It's not hard. She's everywhere. You just ask Her to be here, to sort of concentrate Herself in this one spot, and help you.'

'I'm not sure about this,' Lisa said.

'Do you want to be rid of the brag?' Olly asked. 'When you've got your Goddess invoked, you just keep chanting about Her – how She's good and great, and loving and protective, and asking Her to defeat the thing. You just go on and on chanting and concentrating and the brag shrinks. Gets smaller and smaller. And then we put it in a small box, or can, or bottle. Seal it up. And, traditionally, throw it into the Red Sea.'

'The Red Sea?' Alex said, trying to remember where that was.

'This is weird,' Lisa said. 'I wish I'd never got involved in this.'

'It helps,' Olly said, 'to have more than one person chanting.'

'I don't believe in your "Goddess",' Lisa said.

'Nor me,' Alex said.

'Oh, but you believe in ghosts, though?' Olly shrugged. 'Doesn't really matter what you believe in. Or whether you believe in anything. The Goddess – and the Gods – are there, whether you believe in 'em or not. Always have been. Just *imagine*. Imagine what you'd want a great Goddess to be, if you *did* believe in Her. That'll work just as well. 'Cos I'm with you, and I'm a friend of Hers.'

From upstairs came a crashing of hooves.

'Aye-aye,' Olly said. 'Sounds like we're back in business. You got something to put the brag in once it's shrunk?'

Lisa darted across the room to the bar, went behind it and into a small room. A moment later she came out again with a coffee jar. 'The staff coffee,' she said. 'I just emptied it out.'

Olly took the small, screw-topped jar. 'Cool.' She put the jar on the carpet at her feet and held out her hands to them. 'Let's make a circle.'

Alex and Lisa came and held hands with Olly. 'Goddess, come to us,' Olly began, in her deep, witchy voice. 'Mother of the living, Mother of the dead, come to us –'

Come to us here, in this bar, in this pub, smelling of tobacco and beer, Alex thought, feeling silly. He was glad no one else was there, and very glad none of his friends were there, or he would have been too embarrassed for words.

'Laughing Goddess, weeping Goddess, come to us.' Olly shook Alex's arm. 'Say something.'

'Er – what?'

'Say something.'

'Er – come and give us a hand, Goddess.' He couldn't help but giggle.

'Good. Lise.'

'Help me get rid of this thing!' Lisa said.

'Mother, Goddess, hear our prayers. Come –'

With a crash, the door into the bar flew open, banging against the wall. A rush of wind came in. Alex felt it push against him. Was this brag, he wondered, one of those who *did* hurt people?

'Help us now, Mother, Sister, Daughter, Friend!' Olly cried. 'Bring us Your strength, give us Your protection –'

The brag cantered round them in a circle, passing through tables and chairs when it needed to. Its big paws clopped on the wooden floor. It was in its ridiculous donkeyish shape again, but its muzzle had lengthened and was now toothed like a crocodile's, while its eyes had narrowed and were like stone. It didn't seem as funny as it had earlier.

'Take no notice,' Olly shouted, above the brag's roar. 'Oh Goddess, Mother, protect us –'

'Protect us!' Alex said, with feeling, as the lights went out and he saw the brag's eyes

glowing in the
dark and its teeth
shining in the
light from
its eyes.

The air tingled.
A little buzz, a little
shock, was going from
Olly to him and to Lisa
and back again. He felt
the palms of his hands not just itching, but
tingling, almost stinging. The sensation ran
down his back. His hair stirred. He wondered
if it was standing on end.

'The Goddess is here!' Olly called out.

The brag squealed, cocked up its tail,
turned and bounded away through the bar

door. The lights flickered and came on again, though dimly.

'Petty-fiend, stand!' Olly bellowed and Alex jumped and stared at her. It didn't sound like her voice.

The brag stopped in its tracks, in the doorway, and looked back over one shoulder. Its crocodile teeth had gone and now it looked like a purple donkey that had been caught doing something very wrong and it was pretending to be ashamed.

Olly, still holding hands with Alex and Lisa, pulled them towards the beast. 'The Mother is great and She is good,' Olly said. 'She gives life and She gives death. She brings joy and sorrow. She is All: Mother and Sister, Daughter and Lover. She is –'

It went on and on and seemed to be having no effect at all on the brag, though it did duck its head and seem apprehensive.

'Concentrate, you two!' Olly said. 'Get into it – it's getting a foot free!'

And, indeed, one of the brag's feet was wiggling and trying to kick Lisa.

Alex concentrated. He repeated what Olly was saying and tried to *feel* what the words meant. 'Great Mother –' He remembered a little of what he'd learned about the Greek and Roman goddesses at school. People had once believed in them – what if he'd been one of them? He tried to imagine his mother at her very kindest and best – his mother without any bad temper or sarcasm. It was a stretch, but he tried hard.

'Brings life and death –' She gave everything life: babies, birds, fish, trees, everything. And took away the pain of the old and sick.

He felt himself filling with warmth. It was like growing taller, growing stronger. It was like suddenly being much wiser.

'Look!' Lisa said.

Alex opened his eyes – which he hadn't known he'd closed – and saw that the brag was definitely smaller. Instead of the size of a horse, it was now the size of a large dog.

'Oh Goodess, You who are good,' Olly chanted. 'Guide, Protector, You who love and understand all things –'

Alex repeated the words, and actually saw the brag shrink as he looked at it, dropping from the size of a Labrador to a Pekinese.

'Alex,' Olly said. 'Oh Great Goddess, be with us here – run over and get that jar – You who watch over us all – doesn't matter about letting go hands – the Goddess loves, the Goddess pities – fetch it quick! Oh, Goddess!'

Alex let go of their hands and ran across to where they'd been standing a few minutes before. The lights had come back to full power and the coffee jar was easy to see. He snatched it up and ran back to Olly, unscrewing the lid as he went. He was dismayed, though, to see just how small the mouth of the jar was.

'It's never going to shrink that small!'

'The Goddess is Love, the Goddess is Joy – oh yes, it is – Leaves on the trees, you know how She feels – unscrew it! You have? Good! – Fish in the sea, you know how She feels –'

'Have a heart, Olly!' someone said. It was the brag, now the size of a pink cat. 'I was only playing about!'

Lisa gasped and demanded, 'D'you *know* this brag?'

'Never seen its red, googly eyes before in me life! – Goddess, You are with us! Help us! – Don't listen to it!'

'I'll go away, like you said.' The brag sat up and begged. 'Only don't put me in that jar! Don't throw me in the Red Sea!'

'Can't afford to throw you in the Red Sea, darlin',' Olly said. 'More likely to chuck you in the ornamental pond in Leason's Park. Oh Goddess! Moon shining! Great in Goodness!'

'No! No! Please! Be a sport!' The brag was the size of a rat, and green. Alex started to feel sorry for it.

'Concentrate, please,' Olly said. 'One last big effort – Alex, Lisa. Great Goddess, You are good –'

'You are kind,' Lisa said, getting into the swing of things, now she could see the brag was almost finished. 'You have helped me, and protected me –'

'Goddess, You are powerful,' Alex said, thinking of someone like an Olympic javelin thrower, in a Greek gown, carved from marble.

The brag shrank quite suddenly to the size of a small, orange mouse.

'Aha!' Olly swooped, snatched it up and dropped it into the jar which Alex was holding out. He screwed on the lid, and handed it to Olly.

'Goddess,' said Olly, with tired gratitude, 'thank you.'

'Thank you,' Lisa said.

From her pocket, Olly took a thick marker pen, and drew a strange symbol on the lid of the jar. 'That'll keep it in.'

Alex felt that his head was quieter, less full of buzzing. His hands felt easy, without any itching. 'The place is quiet now,' he said.

'Thank God!' Lisa said.

'Goddess,' said Olly.

Out of the air stepped the Green Lady and the White.

'Now, isn't it much nicer without that nasty thing?' said the Green Lady.

'It is,' the White Lady agreed, 'even with you still around.'

Olly threw the little coffee jar in the air, and everyone flinched, but she caught it. 'All I have to do now, is remember to chuck it in the pond.'

Alex cleared his throat. 'If you like . . . I'll do that for you.'

'Oh – cool,' Olly said, and dropped the jar into his hands.

Alex stood holding it. He could feel the brag moving about inside. He tried to peer in, but couldn't see past the paper wrapper, and he didn't like to tear it off in case Olly thought his interest in the brag was unprofessional.

'Right!' she said. 'I can get you back to your mother before my name's fossilised in mudstone.'

14. To Olly, Alex and Success

The Green Lady threw her arms above her head and shrieked.

Everyone in the crowded bar froze. Hands jerked. Drink spilled from glasses. Heads snapped round.

'Oh my sins, my unconfessed and unforgiven sins!' the Green Lady cried. There she stood, in the middle of the bar. People stared at her, their mouths open.

She held the pose for a moment, holding their attention. Then she lowered her arms with a moan and wrung her hands. 'Oh my sins,' she sobbed on a softer note, as she drifted towards the bar's further door. 'Oh, my unconfessed and unforgiven sins . . .'

Before she reached the door, she faded, melted into the colours of the bar, vanishing.

A din of chatter broke out, a banging down of glasses, a shifting of stools and chairs. People saying:

'Did you see that?'

'I told you!'

'What? I didn't see anything.'

'A ghost!'

'I never thought I'd see –'

'*What?* I didn't see *anything*!'

Two young waitresses came to their table. 'Balti chicken?'

'That's mine!' Kirsty said. She was looking very pretty with her face made up and earrings on. Alex hardly recognized her and he felt quite proud that it was because of him they were having this evening out.

'Three sausage and cheddar mash,' said the other girl, grinning. 'That's Olly!'

'Guilty as charged – hand it over!' Olly was all dressed up in her motorbike gear again, with her crash helmet and gauntlets under her chair. She'd arrived, with a lot of noise and dust, on Stormrider. Her earrings this evening – Alex always looked at her earrings now – were little, silver, double-headed axes.

The other plates were handed round and one of the waitresses bent down and said to Lisa, 'Just taken another booking for the Haunted Room Special!'

'Oh?' Lisa said. 'When?'

'Couple of months' time.'

With a big smile, Lisa looked round at her guests. 'The phone's ringing off the hook. We're full for the Bank Holiday weekend!'

'Good for you!' Rob said.

'A toast,' Lisa said. 'To Olly and Alex and success!'

Kirsty, Rob and Lisa all raised their glasses. 'To Olly, Alex and success!'

Alex felt himself blushing. Olly said, 'Speech, Alex, speech!'

'Oh, leave him alone,' Lisa said.

'So kind of you to ask us along,' Kirsty said. 'It's lovely to have a weekend away. But . . . You haven't – ?'

Rob said, 'You haven't put us in the room the Green Lady haunts?'

'Oh *no*,' Lisa said. 'You're in the White Lady's room. *Much* quieter. In fact, there's a lovely couple from London in the Green Lady's tonight. They're having the Haunted Room Special. Phoned from London and asked for the Green Lady. Oh!' Lisa looked dismayed. 'You wouldn't prefer an ordinary room, would you? Without a ghost at all? Only I thought –'

'We would,' Kirsty said firmly.

'Every time,' said Rob.

'I *never*,' said Kirsty, stabbing her fork into a piece of chicken, 'never want anything to do with ghosts – or goblins, or brags, or bogles, or long-leggeddy beasties – ever again in my whole life. Not if I live to be a hundred and five.'

Which made Alex think, uneasily, of the coffee jar in his bedside cabinet, with the brag inside it. He'd told his mother that he'd thrown it in the pond in the park. He'd told Olly that he'd thrown it in the pond in the park. But he hadn't.

He was thinking of taking it to school with him. He was thinking, in particular, of Mrs Witty's next maths lesson. And of what might happen if, in the middle of it, he unscrewed the coffee jar's lid . . .